Lilus Kikus

and Other Stories

by Elena Poniatowska

Elena Poniatowska in 1963

Lilus Kikus

and Other Stories

by Elena Poniatowska

TRANSLATION AND INTRODUCTION BY

Elizabeth Coonrod Martínez

DRAWINGS BY

Leonora Carrington

UNIVERSITY OF NEW MEXICO PRESS ◆ ALBUQUERQUE

11 10 09 08 07 06 05   1 2 3 4 5 6 7

LIBRARY OF CONGRESS CATALOGING-IN-PUBLICATION DATA

Poniatowska, Elena.
Lilus Kikus and other stories / by Elena Poniatowska ;
translation and introduction by Elizabeth Coonrod Martínez ;
drawings by Leonora Carrington.
p. cm.
Includes bibliographical references.
ISBN 0-8263-3582-9 (pbk. : alk. paper)
1. Poniatowska, Elena—Translations into English.
I. Martínez, Elizabeth Coonrod II. Title.
PQ7297.P63A26 2005
863'.64—dc22
2005014034

Drawings by Leonora Carrington,
used by permission of Elena Poniatowska

Book design and type composition by Kathleen Sparkes
This book is typeset using Utopia 10/15, 23P6
Display type is Frutiger

This book is dedicated to the beautiful

young women who are my nieces:

Julie, Margaret, Tish, Candace,

Nikki, and Dani

E. C. M.

C O N T E N T S

Introduction

As the translation of the satirical novel *Lilus Kikus* and accompanying stories goes to press, I am aware that—despite her distinction as one of Mexico's most prolific and greatest contemporary writers—there are potential English-language readers who will ask, Who is Elena Poniatowska? She herself reacted to my recent reference to her as Mexico's "grand dame of letters" with humility and a statement that she is undeserving of such tribute. And yet she has been a leading voice of Mexico for five decades, beginning as a newspaper interviewer with provocative questions and continuing as a perceptive chronicler of the contemporary Mexican—especially the Mexican woman.

Poniatowska has excelled in several genres—as journalist, novelist, short-story writer, and essayist. She possesses a significant talent for revealing the light, personal side of the human being in her interviews, and her fiction focuses on the search for identity and meaning in human existence more than on plot. Her political writing began with wry observations of those often not revealed by the hegemonical leadership—those who do not rise to power, who are used by others, and who constitute the working force of the nation. It is only in the United States that Poniatowska is not as well known as other, more recent Mexican women writers—women whose novels entertain with food preparations and sexual adventures as they retell Mexican history. Poniatowska broke into publishing when few women dared or found it possible to emerge among a male-dominated literary establishment. Her oeuvre—numerous publications of nonfiction as well as fiction—is an enduring and consistent sociopolitical commitment to people whose voices would not otherwise be heard.

Who is Elena Poniatowska? Her publications (whether newspaper essays, prologues, or her own books) have created her reputation, but the writer's own humble attitude and generous giving of her time also make her remarkable. Born in 1932, Poniatowska is now at the zenith of her career (although she still has numerous writing projects under way). Her very first publication, the short novel *Lilus Kikus*, occurred in 1954, at about the same time as her entry into journalism, and established a model for her works to follow. What is remarkable about this story is that it was created by a young woman with no college training, only beginning her writing career, who nevertheless crafted a humorous and somber reflection on how little girls were raised in 1940s society. Poniatowska employs sharp tools of satire to weave meaning between the lines, a strategy that would go unrecognized for years.

In an era when only men were considered great writers, Poniatowska was merely credited with writing a cute children's book, and remained on the sidelines of "intellectual" life, unrelenting and prolific in her writing and research until years later when literary awards and journalistic prizes began to accumulate. Poniatowska has cited as an influence Rosario Castellanos's (1925–1974) master's thesis on the status of women, which was published in 1950, and Elena Garro's (1920–1998) stories, first published in 1962. These are the only other two women writers who published in mid-twentieth-century Mexico, and neither was embraced by Mexican intellectual society.

Poniatowska has been an influence on and coach of other women in writing workshops that she has conducted since 1983, when they were founded as part of the Interdisciplinary Program for Women's Studies at Mexico City's prestigious private university, Colegio de México. Some of her students are now renowned authors themselves, among them Silvia Molina and Rosa Nissán. Poniatowska is one of the originators of and a regular contributor to the magazine *fem*, Mexico's first feminist periodical (founded in 1976),which has endured despite occasional setbacks, including the disappearance and death of its editor, Alaide Foppa. Many intellectual Mexican women initially tried to avoid such feminist associations for fear of censorship of their work. Poniatowska has also contributed to Mexican artistic life with her participation in the creation of the publishing venture Editorial Siglo Veintiuno, and the founding of a national film library, Cineteca Nacional.

Principally and foremost, however, Poniatowska is a writer. First, she is responsible for creating and transforming the interview genre in Mexico. Her early claim to fame is that she interviewed the rich and famous and revealed a side of them not previously known. She is a keen observer, and this talent is revealed as much in her journalism and nonfiction as in her fiction. After her entry into journalism with interviews of famous personages, Poniatowska has been persistent in seeking to represent those who are different and in providing a medium for their voices. For some fifty years, she has continued to contribute articles to newspapers and magazines. Her books of nonfiction deal with a variety of themes: the voices of the mothers of political prisoners disappeared by government forces as they clamped down on public political activity during the mid-twentieth century (*Fuerte es el silencio*, 1980); the voices of those who have no home and defy the government with their squatter's initiatives (also in *Fuerte es el silencio*, 1980); the inept and delayed rescue efforts by the government following the 1985 Mexico City earthquake (*Nada, nadie*, 1988; *Nothing, Nobody*, 1995); the story of a young girl with cerebral palsy who, as she becomes an adult, fulfills her desire to live life as fully as possible, even adopting a child (*Gaby Brimmer*, 1979); and the story of a thirteen-year-old's rape and her fortitude in denouncing an unjust legal system (*Las mil y una . . . [la herida de Paulina]*, 2000). A recent book celebrates seven talented and avant-garde women artists, several of whom have received scant critical attention (*Las siete cabritas*, 2000).

Poniatowska's introductory essays to art books, which are numerous, capture beauty in words, also saluting the artists or a particular region of Mexico. Her essay accompanying a collection of photographs by Graciela Iturbide of the women of the Oaxaca region is a tantalizing portrait to match Iturbide's work. (While the original book has gone out of print, its story and photographs have been republished, with other Poniatowska narratives, in *Luz, luna y lunitas*.) Poniatowska notes that it was the women of Juchitán, Oaxaca, who renewed Tina Modotti's love of life, and her words in this portrait pay tribute to these women, who have endured invasions, modernity, and politics. Their men, meanwhile, adore them. This is Poniatowska's narrative at its most delicious, quite different from her many narratives that depict the abuse of women by rape, violence, and poverty.

Poniatowska is an intuitive interviewer, always finding a respectful way to approach subjects from all walks of life. In her fiction, however, like other writers of her generation, she is an intellectual more than an intuitive writer. Her novels, full of angst and meaning, often reveal the stories of women forgotten or ignored by the power system in their society: a *soldadera* and wife of a soldier during the Mexican Revolution who is denied her widow's pension by the new government and spends the rest of her life in a marginal existence in the rapidly growing Mexico City (*Here's to you, Jesusa*); a wife left behind by a famous artist who grieves and strives to find her identity—this text is also an interesting examination of the lack of value put on women's lives as compared to men's in Mexican society—(*Dear Diego*); a spirited woman who fights against political regimes and for the worker (*Tinísima*); and a wealthy woman who seeks an understanding of life and tries to help those less fortunate (*Paseo de la Reforma*, not yet published in translation). Her most recent novel (*The Skin of the Sky*) focuses on the history of modern astronomy in Mexico and examines changes in government and society during most of the twentieth century. Here science serves as a principal character, personified by the male astronomer who becomes increasingly frustrated over internal and external impediments to progress but remains immature and chauvinistic in his understanding of women. Poniatowska's most recent publication of fiction is a new collection of short stories (*Tlapalería*) that reveals a gallery of snapshots of contemporary young people. Some face life in poverty and on the street, as well as drug addiction, and others embark on existential quests for meaning through the myths of their society. As we expect of Poniatowska, the stories offer the subtle message of the devaluing of female life as well as an astute use of colloquial, contemporary Mexican Spanish.

In an era of very limited access to publishing for women—the 1950s through the 1970s—Poniatowska emerged as a subtly present female voice in a male-focused society (although regularly and sweetly referred to in diminutive fashion as "Elenita").

She cloaked her persistent pushing of the buttons of those in power with the sweetness she was assigned. But she never relented. Hired in 1953 as a society reporter (thanks to family connections), she set herself a goal of submitting one interview per day. This sharpened her writing and interviewing skills as well as satisfying newspaper editors, who then allowed her to interview subjects for reasons other than "gossip." By carefully building her experience and creating opportunities for other assignments, she went on to steady journalistic coverage.

During the 1960s, Poniatowska established a regular routine of Sunday visits to a principal Mexico City prison in order to talk to family members visiting imprisoned relatives. She quietly gained access, however, to the very victims of government brutality and to information not allowed in newspapers by the Mexican regime. The government regularly censored the media, but Poniatowska found a way to reveal information by dropping it as tidbits into her newspaper stories. When the 1968 student demonstration and government massacre occurred, jailers were accustomed to her routine of Sunday visits and granted her access when other reporters were not allowed. Thus, she was able to compile and publish the important book *La noche de Tlatelolco* (1971; *Massacre in Mexico*, 1992). Although a one-day incident is the focus, community activism had built up over several months to protest increasing government repression. Student groups hoped to gain international attention to their cause with the arrival of numerous athletes and journalists as Mexico hosted the Olympics in late October of 1968. On October 2, following a peaceful demonstration, the Mexican government bore down on the Plaza de las Tres Culturas in the neighborhood of Tlatelolco with tanks, helicopters, and snipers on the roofs of buildings, killing hundreds of people. President Gustavo Díaz Ordaz, however, immediately accused the students of inciting a riot. In her text, Poniatowska contrasts government-censored newspaper reports with the testimony and direct quotes of those imprisoned, and from the family members of the disappeared and unaccounted for after the massacre.

While Poniatowska's journalistic writing gained momentum, she continued to publish fiction that revealed the plight and subjective consciousness of women in her society. By 1980, her two collections of short stories and three novels—*Lilus Kikus*; *Here's to You, Jesusa*; and *Dear Diego*—demonstrate an intellectual analysis, depicted through women, that was not being pursued by any other writer in her society. Works by women writers Elena Garro and Rosario Castellanos had paved the way for some of this discourse, but by the early 1970s Garro was exiled from Mexico for political reasons and Castellanos had died.

Poniatowska has even gazed across the border at the fiction of Mexican-heritage women, or Chicanas, in the United States. Her interest in the U.S. Chicana narratives that reached wide audiences in the 1980s led her to publish a translation into Spanish of Sandra Cisneros's first novel, *The House on Mango Street*. In a journalistic essay in the Mexican newspaper *La Jornada* in 1993, Poniatowska declared that Chicana writers were leading the way back to cultural icons and empowering women's images in Mexican folklore and culture.

To imagine an English-language version of Poniatowska, one would have to create a composite of several figures: in the area of journalism, the interviewing trailblazer Barbara Walters, for her poignant, at times intrusive and coy but always persistent questioning of famous subjects; and the "new journalist" Joan Didion, for her intensely subjective analyses and revelations of the underdog in political economies and/or the outcasts of those in power. Among fiction writers, two comparable authors are Anne Tyler, for her psychological evaluation of characters and portrayals of their domestic worlds; and Margaret Atwood, for her introspective child and female characters, and intense probing of girls' and women's inner psyches.

Poniatowska's constant tactic, whether in journalistic or creative writing, is that of not overtly stating what she sees represented in her society, instead reflecting it between the lines, or in collages of fluid narrative and reporting style. With these subtle strategies, she has consistently revealed the voices of those disenfranchised or erased by their society. And probably because Poniatowska's approach was not overt or aggressive, she has been able to advance a feminist stance.

Her work has been analyzed and studied in recent critical texts and anthologies of Latin American and Mexican women writers, as well as in one book-length study. Poniatowska has received numerous literature awards, notably the Premio Mazatlán for her novel *Hasta no verte, Jesús mío* (1969; *Here's To You, Jesusa*, 2001), and again in 1992 for the novel *Tinísima* (1992; *Tinísima*, 1994), based loosely on Tina Modotti's life. Recent important literary awards include Spain's Premio Alfaguara best novel of the year award, for *La piel del cielo* (*The Skin of the Sky*), and Mexico's National Prize for Literature (now called Sciences and Art), both in 2002. The previous year the nations of Colombia and Chile both saluted this Mexican writer with their highest writing awards. It should be noted that Poniatowska's publishing record was achieved through her own efforts, largely without the help of an agent to introduce her work around the world. Only recently did a U.S. literary agent, Susan Bergholz, secure English translation and publication of some of Poniatowska's recent novels with the distinguished New York house Farrar, Straus & Giroux.

Poniatowska's journalism prizes in Mexico are also extensive. She was awarded but refused (in protest against the

Mexican government for the student massacre in 1968) the Xavier Villaurrutia prize for her book *La noche de Tlatelolco* (1971; *Massacre in Mexico*, 1992). In 1978 she was honored with the National Prize in Journalism, and has received other top awards for journalistic writing, including the Manuel Buendía prize (1987), the Coatlicue prize for women's issues (1990), the Premio Nacional Juchimán (1993), and the National Prize for Cultural Journalism (1994).

While Poniatowska's acclaim in Mexico has been steadfast and respectful during the past two decades, her notice in the United States has been relatively recent. She is well known, however, in academic circles. An honorary member of the Modern Language Association—a form of recognition bestowed on only a few international writers—she has been granted honorary doctorates by two Florida universities, Columbia University in New York City, and by the national universities of Sinaloa and Toluca in Mexico.

The most striking aspect of Poniatowska's fiction is the voice of the female, long denied its place in the Mexican hegemony. Her child character Lilus seems to evolve into the woman deserted by her spouse of ten years in *Querido Diego, te abraza Quiela* (1978; *Dear Diego*, 1986), who manages to evolve in the course of the novel to recover her sense of personhood. The character Quiela of *Dear Diego* emerges stronger and with different experiences in *Tinísima* and *Paseo de la reforma* (1999). Thus, the female voice, and the essence of Poniatowska's meditation on the female in her society, is launched in the short novel *Lilus Kikus* of 1954 and the stories (published in collections in 1967 and 1979) provided in translation here. They contain the traits and thematics of Poniatowska's entire body of work—her keen observation of human beings and her preoccupation with people's treatment of one another within their society. The stories included here were selected for their exploration of a theme similar to that of *Lilus Kikus*, that of the female seeking identity and meaning in her society, long before the 1980s when many women writers burst onto the publishing scene with strong female characters.

Lilus Kikus can be read on several levels. On a first or superficial level, it is a cute children's story (as it was interpreted in its day by Mexican critics). A more thorough reading reveals a meditation on the hows and whys of society's patriarchal rules (enforced by both men and women, religious and political authorities) for little girls and women. And a new reading can startle with the violent underlying tension of the final chapters, and the ultimate brainwashing (or not?) of a spirited girl. These multiple levels of readings demonstrate Poniatowska' early talent for subversive writing.

In one of the few studies of *Lilus Kikus*, published in 1983, Juan Bruce-Novoa notes the child character's preference for the traditional domain of men. As the first chapter opens, Lilus plays in the grassy area in front of her house and near the street, where she can observe cars and the many people walking by. She participates in a space that is public space, not enclosed or isolated within the home, as women are traditionally supposed to do. Lilus plays doctor—a male profession—practicing medicine on various fruits. Later she climbs the wall in her backyard to talk to the philosopher next door. When she is on vacation in Acapulco, she goes into town and joins a political demonstration.

Despite its enchanting and humorous descriptions, the story of Lilus is not a happy tale, as Bruce-Novoa points out, and yet it continues to be cited in Mexico as a light children's story. Critics and prestigious writers such as Carlos Monsiváis, Juan Rulfo, and Carlos Fuentes have failed to notice Poniatowska's subtle accomplishment. They categorized *Lilus Kikus* as a children's story; the author herself never did, and none of her subsequent work is categorized as children's literature. It should have been recognized for its ability to convey powerful, provocative ideas and statements in short sentences and paragraphs, an avant-garde style well suited to political satire.

The short novel is modeled on the traditional coming-of-age story or European *Bildungsroman* in which the character attends a boarding school (or serves an apprenticeship) to learn a trade and/or the rules of society, has various adventures in which both right and wrong are discerned, and is finally prepared to assume adult life. Poniatowska's novel ends with Lilus having learned the conventions of her society and how to prepare for her role: to be patient, submissive, and dignified as a wife, and to choose a spouse with an honorable profession. A street peddler or a gardener is not desirable, while a millionaire is (Poniatowska is obviously indicating those at the helm of her country). She is also taught not to judge adultery too quickly. Traditional sex roles and double standards are the future of the little girl Lilus, not to mention the possibility of death at the hands of her spouse, as occurs with Lilus's friend Chiruelita. Religious schooling plays a role in Lilus's education for the purpose of instilling obedience and social oppression. The Bible story or parable related in the final chapter enforces fear and punishment for disobedience, and Lilus acknowledges having learned to follow the "signs." But what are these "signs"? Do they represent the rigid rules of a patriarchal society, or possible subversive signs that the young author has deftly learned to adapt to her use? This novel leaves the answer open.

The traditional coming-of-age story featured a male character and part of his life apprenticeship included sexual awakening and a learning experience with a "bad" woman, followed by the understanding of securing a "good" woman—virgin—for a wife. Insert a female character and the traditional plot is complicated. But Poniatowska deftly turns the tables on her society's morality training with an alternative character. The good girl Lilus prepares—as a virgin trained by the nuns—to become a wife. The bad girl or "black sheep" in the novel suffers expulsion from school because she defiles her "lily"—literally and symbolically. Her sexual experience is obvious as she talks to Lilus. Lilus asks Laura Lamb, her "black sheep" friend, to tell her what she has learned, and the creative word play that ensues indicates she is likely pregnant; hence her expulsion rather than simple punishment for her conduct during the religious procession. Later, in a dream, Lilus will ask about Mary Magdalene and how one becomes an adulteress. Moralistic women with the word *prohibited* painted in black on their chests state that they are there to save her, but Lilus insists that she is not lost. At this and several other junctures in these short chapters, Poniatowska's feminist voice is loud and clear. Her contemplation of nuns in black as symbols of restrictive religious training, as alternatives to the shame of those who are not virgins, recurs in such short stories as "Happiness."

While *Lilus Kikus* is a delightful read—with apt and humorous descriptions and observations of members of Lilus's society—the chapters descend to a darker space where a little girl is no longer free and adventurous but accepting of male social order, a conclusion that is available, among others, to the reader. As Bruce-Novoa points out, the statement at the end of the novel that Lilus learns to "believe in signs" is purposefully ambiguous. She could have been trained or convinced to fear God and to accept a male code of signs or patriarchy, in which case the ending would signify the young woman's silence of conformity. But it could also indicate discreet and quiet rejection—by manipulation or deconstruction—of the Mexican code of signification.

In essence, the young writer Poniatowska found a way to talk back to her society in 1954 by disguising her commentary in a quasi-children's story. It was not an era when "in your face" or direct political tactics would have served a woman writer. *Lilus Kikus* holds up a mirror to represent female repression in Mexican society. Male observers saw this character as cute and attractive like Poniatowska's character Esmeralda in "You Arrive by Nightfall." The critical community would not discover Poniatowska's true accomplishments until years later, after her corpus of work demonstrated continuity in the revelation of women's voices and roles in society, together with the need for respect and justice for women. As Bruce-Novoa observes, *Lilus Kikus* prefigures all of Poniatowska's later work, whether as interviewer of important personages or chronicler of women's lives in her fiction.

A recent study by Sara Poot Herrera suggests the convent school as a place of solitude, a place Lilus comes to love just as Poniatowska the writer learns to prefer—and choose—the cloister of a writing life. Thus, as with many writers' early works, this short novel demonstrates a writer choosing her path. Poniatowska was informing her society that she herself had chosen her role rather than accepting the one imposed on women (despite the superficial evidence of Lilus accepting that path). Poot Herrera sees the curiosity of this little-girl character and her many questions to the adults in her life as interrogations of Mexican society of the kind that flow throughout Poniatowska's writings. Lilus's questions merge into the demands, issues, and controversies of later characters. Thus, *Lilus Kikus* initiates, metaphorically and chronologically, Elena Poniatowska's body of work.

Biographical information will shed some light on the author's literary creation. Poniatowska was born in Paris, the daughter of a Frenchman of Polish origin, Evremont Poniatowski Sperry, and the French-born daughter of Mexican parents, Dolores Amor Iturbide. (She explains that in Polish tradition, an *i* is placed at the end of the last name if the person is of male gender, and an *a* if of female gender; hence her last name is slightly different from her father's.) She and her sister were raised in France, where her parents took part in the French resistance effort early in World War II. In 1942, however, her mother took the two girls to Mexico to escape the war. Here Elena discovered her mother's Mexican nationality for the first time (some of this biographical data is included in the novel *La flor de Lis*, currently untranslated). Her mother's affluent family required that her daughters be educated in private schools and taught in English and French. Elena's father later joined the family in Mexico, and a younger brother, Jan, was born in 1947. He unfortunately lost his life in a car accident in 1968. Poniatowska became a naturalized citizen in 1969.

Baptized Hélène Elizabeth Louise Amélie Paula Dolores in traditional European Catholic fashion, Poniatowska's life followed the dictates of European tradition only during her childhood. Her career as the future chronicler of Mexican society likely began as she sought to learn the Spanish language from the maids in her household; her work demonstrates a keen ear for colloquial Mexican Spanish. Trips to Acapulco or to a relative's ranch are likely to have occurred during her young life, and are depicted for the character Lilus. As a teenager, Poniatowska studied at the Sacred Heart Convent School near Philadelphia (similar to the school described in the final chapter of *Lilus Kikus*) for two years, a type of finishing school where wealthy Catholic girls were prepared for marriage and life as an obedient wife and socialite. Her family's financial constraints prevented Poniatowska from pursuing a college degree in the United

States, so she returned to Mexico City. She found a writing coach in Juan José Arreola (who launched a series for new writers, *Los presentes*, with *Lilus Kikus*, also publishing Carlos Fuentes and other new writers) and access to a newspaper job through her family's acquaintances. As she attended high society social events with her family, she used the opportunity to meet people she would interview in the near future.

An additional item of information also helps us understand her assessment of roles for women in her society. Poniatowska had a child out of wedlock (through no choice of her own) and traveled to France to give birth to a son at about the same time as the publication of *Lilus Kikus*. Years later, she married Guillermo Haro, who adopted her first son and with whom she had a son and a daughter. This information adds significance to the subtle references to virginity and pregnancy in *Lilus Kikus*.

Although this first novel may read like a collection of stories featuring the character Lilus, close attention reveals subtle connections between chapters. The sequence becomes more intense and conclusive as each chapter proceeds. In the first chapter, Lilus does not possess dolls; she is not a traditional girl child. She prefers observing people and thinking about her society and what makes it tick. In the second chapter, she notes people's characteristics and habits, and how they can dictate their assessments of others. In chapter three, in Acapulco, she feels pretty; she has entered puberty. By chapter four, she wishes to participate in politics and finds herself used and admired. In chapter five her imagination is fully employed as she contemplates not only the sunlight and dust particles, but also her father's routines and rigidity. She also asks the maid about the nature of kisses. In chapter six, she imagines her soul like the rooms of a house; she tries to make herself a better person. In the end her inner being remains "impregnated" by the occupant. Thoughts on kisses and impregnation lead to the discovery of the soiled virgin in chapter seven. The Lamb is expelled because of her sexual behavior and possible pregnancy in chapter eight, and Lilus dreams about Mary Magdalene in the next chapter while she is sick with a fever. The moralist women call her a "gluttonous virgin" and tell her she is not an angelic being as her mother thinks. In chapter ten, Lilus tells her neighbor about the Lamb. He identifies her as the "free thinker," the "feminist," and Lilus replies, "exactly." The little girl who worries that she only gets "halfway" in previous chapters is suddenly more resolute about the issues in her society. At the end of this chapter, her mother tells her she needs to "learn to discover your own answers," and that is exactly what she is doing. She has just provided several possibilities to the philosopher-neighbor, and she provides reasons for her friend Chiruelita's behavior in the penultimate chapter. Lilus "knows of the dangers that await those who attempt to speak well," and prefers to be quiet (or subtle). Here the author shows, rather than tells, what happens to women if they remain in a "dummy," juvenile state. This is a significant and strong chapter prior to the final chapter where the character seems to be the younger Lilus again, afraid and then marveling at her discovery of the nuns and the convent school. She has revealed her own answers, she has reasons and examples, but in the end she chooses to follow the traditional path. Or so it would seem to the inattentive reader/critic.

The character Lilus may seemingly accept defeat at the end of the novel, but Poniatowska the writer never does, a fact that becomes more and more evident in her subsequent stories and novels. *Lilus Kikus* is invaluable as a foreshadowing of the mature Poniatowska—it provides insight into her political inclinations and the beginning of an acute contemplation of gender and Mexican society. Readers should remember that it was written and published in the mid-twentieth century, an era not open to women stepping out of traditional roles. It reveals the budding talent of a woman who has become one of Mexico's greatest writers.

Although *Lilus Kikus* has been continuously reprinted in new editions, little critical commentary has appeared (and almost none in Mexico). Poniatowska did not publish any other fiction until 1967, when her book titled *Los cuentos de Lilus Kikus* appeared, which included the short novel again and twelve additional stories divided into three sections. Three stories from this publication are included here: "La hija del filósofo" ("The Philosopher's Daughter"), "Canto quinto" ("Fifth Call"), and "La felicidad" ("Happiness"). She published her first novels—on the soldadera of the Mexican Revolution in 1969, and on the deserted wife in 1978—between her two collections of short stories. The final story included here, "De noche vienes" ("You Arrive by Nightfall"), is from her 1979 short-story collection *De noche vienes*. Although this story appeared during the feminist awakening of the 1970s, it was likely written many years earlier. The principal character, Esmeralda, is a fresh, healthy, alluring woman with a respectable profession, that of a nurse. She smiles sweetly and regularly, and appears not to catch the comments of sexual innuendo delivered by the judge who accuses her of bigamy. In fact, her case is a direct challenge to male authority (and an apt metaphor of Poniatowska and her chosen career). The story makes excellent use of dialogue, with a somewhat ambiguous denouement.

It was completely distorted, however, in the film directed by Jaime Humberto Hermosillo nearly twenty years later. The film diminished the story's subtle denunciation of a society where men can have outside lovers but women are arrested and sentenced in court for doing the same, instead making the story into a homosexual romp. The 1997 film *De noche vienes* grossly alters the structure of Poniatowska's story, using flashbacks to demonstrate Esmeralda's life, as well as creating scenes of sexual behavior not depicted in the story. The film also featured considerable nudity, rendering it unsuitable for many viewers. Hermosillo's film received little critical or popular attention, perhaps because of its near-pornographic images and campy exaggerations. Poniatowska herself complained that the lead character was portrayed as a Marilyn Monroe–type figure, which did not make sense to her. The story of a woman who is married to five men at once—and sees no wrong in this—is scandalous and a definite affront to the Mexican patriarchal system. It is a shame the same story was not represented in film. It is a scintillating read, however, with excellent cinematographic descriptions. Esmeralda's observations are acute and precise, and reminiscent of Poniatowska's descriptions in her journalism. The character's personal evaluation of her society is revealed with each observation of the people and objects around her.

In my translation, I hoped to retain the sense of how Mexican society addresses and categorizes women, so I used *madam* for *señora*—the manner in which married women are addressed—and kept *de* before the last name of each of her spouses, which is the traditional practice, and literally means this woman is now "of" or belongs to this man, e.g., Esmeralda Loyden de Lugo.

Each of Poniatowska's stories selected to accompany the short novel *Lilus Kikus* was chosen for its exploration of the female consciousness—the desire to find meaning in a society that does not consider women important. Thus, I think the stories grow naturally out of Poniatowska's first piece of fiction, demonstrating her early feminist political awareness and a creative affront to patriarchal society that few other women writers risked until the 1980s. Having described the last story first, I will return to the order in which these four stories appear.

"The Philosopher's Daughter" is a feminist spin on the traditional fairy tale, using the language of philosophical discourse. It is important to bear in mind that this story was published in 1967, a decade prior to most feminist activity or publications in Mexico. A young character sits quietly awaiting her father's orders for food or drink as he entertains his male students with long philosophical conversations. Her assigned place is a dark hallway off the principal room, and her days are lonely and tedious. She passes time stitching cloth covers onto her father's books; he seems to feel no affection for her or interest in her life. When an intellectual dispute arises between her father and one of his students, the young man suddenly becomes aware of the girl sitting outside the room and decides to seduce her in order to punish her father. She is afraid at first, then finds his attentions flattering and is drawn into escapades with him. When he arrives for sessions with her father and the other students, she politely pretends they do not have secret encounters, and her father never suspects. One day the student reveals his intellectual power. The philosopher salutes the young upstart, the daughter sees that he is honored and keeps quiet about her "error," and the story continues until he departs the group.

Poniatowska's character—only called "girl" and "the daughter"—represents the plight of the unimportant female, an entity to be controlled by either father or lover. On one occasion the girl attempts a comment pertinent to the group's discussion, but her father yells at her to be quiet and not interfere. She is not allowed to engage in intellectual discussion with her father's students and is defenseless when exposed to the seductive and manipulative ways of the young male. The father is oblivious to anything the girl does other than waiting on him. The story concludes with the philosopher's loss of power and the departure of the young man in victorious triumph. The philosopher sees his daughter for the first time, but does nothing; she returns to her chores as the intellectual group reconvenes. All that matters in this particular patriarchal society are men's victories and defeat. What will become of the daughter? The answer is left open and ambiguous as in *Lilus Kikus*. Poniatowska's language in this story is clever, often leading the reader in one direction and then abruptly changing mid-sentence as suspense ebbs and flows. Her purposeful use of philosophical language, ironic metaphors, and personification is extremely creative and reminiscent of early-twentieth-century avant-garde writing.

"Fifth Call" appears to be a story of ardent love shared by a young couple without a place of their own. But it actually reveals just the opposite—that there is no place for love in their society. The young woman intuits this but her lover cannot see it, as he does not seem to understand her desperate wish to save what they can of love before it crumbles. Even their lovemaking space is alienating: a tiny hotel room with only a bed, a mirror on the wall, and a tiny bathroom with no door. Each wall is of a different strident color, which seems to connect to Julia's nervous sense of reality. She is keenly aware of footsteps in the hallway and an irascible fist banging on the door next to their room (because a guest is abusing his hour's stay). She muses that she and Rodrigo never stay too long; he always has an appointment, something to rush to. As they dress, she thinks about other places they have sought for their lovemaking, and one they nearly rented but which Rodrigo, despite saying they needed to "get organized" and find a place, never really wanted badly enough. He was happy with just saying, "I'll give you a holler."

Julia knows that she is the one who needs to call out, even scream with animalistic energy. She knows their love will not last; she tells him, "I do nothing to save myself." Rodrigo tries to understand what she is saying, but he is incapable. He will never be able to understand her desire for acknowledgment because he has not experienced denial of one's gender and role in society as a woman has. As they leave the tiny room and walk out of the building, she looks back to read the neon sign *Hotel Solitude*—an appropriate metaphor for their relationship. The extreme sensitivity and awareness of this female character evokes woman's desire for communication in a social context. The character quietly screams for acknowledgment. In the end, she will leave knowing, as she has all along, that their love cannot last, that Rodrigo cannot communicate or understand. Their relationship is restricted to occasional encounters in a hotel room, and their walks down Mexico City streets, when they hold hands, but Julia desires an enduring spiritual connection. This character could be the young adult Lilus, who embarks on life in a city she loves, instead of marriage. She longs for under-standing of herself and her place in society. The dialogue be-tween the two lovers is sweet, interspersed with Julia's thoughts about their relationship and remembrances of other, similar encounters. Julia's final statement, barely audible and seemingly to herself, articulates the need for meaning in life: "Get un-dressed, my love, for we are going to die."

The next story, "Happiness," much like "The Philosopher's Daughter," has an excellent rhythm for reading aloud. Its steady flow of escalating tension, with phrases controlled by commas and occasional long, ongoing bursts of emotion, establishes a sense of anxiety. It is also an alternative to the experience of the couple in "Fifth Call" in that these lovers have a small apartment of their own where they can meet regularly. This female character, however, appears more unsure, constantly contradicting herself, telling him she understands his point of view and that he is right, although her inner voice tells her differently. Poniatowska's story is told all in one paragraph, with seemingly endless sentences, separated by comma after comma. I have tried to follow a format better suited to English, with occasional paragraphs, separated by changes in theme. But my attempt was to retain the vulnerable sense of stream-of-consciousness, ongoing exploration by the female character.

In "Happiness," the young woman shares a room or small flat with her lover. Her thoughts take place in bed after their love-making, when he escapes her by falling asleep, even after asking, "Are you there?" to which her response opens the story. The unnamed narrator embarks on a monologue of affirmations to their love: yes, I am right here; yes, of course I love you. She states what he does not, and his negativity seems to incite her persistent affirmations of love. As she points out, he never calls her *dear*, *darling*, or *sweetie*. He tires of her words, like *happiness*. He tells her no one belongs to anyone; isn't the miracle of their love enough? She assures him she believes this, but her thoughts tell another story. Her angst leads to musings about their encounters; the toys he bought in the park, which decorate their room; the neighbor; her youth, lack of experience, and religious upbringing. That day she is stimulated by his unexpected early arrival, excited to leave her loneliness behind, but as soon as the lovemaking ends she feels herself reverting back to where she was. The story, told in extensive monologue, accelerates in tension as the character attempts to stave off her feelings of emptiness. In desperation, she decides she will dress and go out walking to drive herself to exhaustion. The monologue becomes a long, racing diatribe, with ebbs and flows and an explosion of emotion—similar to a buildup in sexual tension—followed by thoughts that culminate in the inevitable understanding that each is forever and inextricably alone, or perhaps, on his or her own in this life.

This nameless character is afraid. She has exposed her inner being, given herself to her lover, and now she wants to find an explanation for her state. Although he has only fallen asleep, she knows he no longer belongs to her and cannot take her with him. You promised always to be with me, she says, realizing that his promises cannot be kept; they are a "couple," she with her head resting on his chest like a medallion. She feels pierced with loneliness, identifying with the paper butterflies he pierced onto the wall to decorate their room. The character thinks about the Catholic training girls receive and is conscious of the foreboding with which it clouded her choices in life. In her mind, she tells the nuns that she likes thorns as well as roses, she enjoys moving out to the prickly side of life (this is an alternative path for Lilus). At one juncture her monologue is a play on the Lord's Prayer as she describes their lover's nest and the enclosure and protection she wants it to provide. She makes several allusions to the "virgin" state of their love, of her skin, of her own experience. This subtle analogy reveals the young woman's sexual awakening, the process of becoming a woman. But she describes herself as strong, her teeth like tools. She wishes she had met her lover (who may be much older) when she was older because her experience might be different, and yet she acknowledges that she still would have to sit and wait for him. As she makes these assessments of her experience—her discovery of life—she consistently asks him what he thinks, but he is asleep and cannot (or will not) respond. The young woman's interior monologue—her own words and interpretations—help give her the strength to combat human solitude or to make decisions about herself. The character who seems at first to be an insecure young woman gains the strong voice of a woman who will prevail and succeed on her own terms.

Although "Happiness" (which the female character tries to grasp, and which eludes her) is a story about a romantic relationship, its narrator demonstrates how small and insignificant she becomes when placed in the traditional construct of the "couple." She must escape the idea that this is happiness, and talks her way to sanity during a dialogue with herself, confronting loneliness (and judgment) and overcoming it. The character's interior reservoir is stronger than she realized, stronger than the outside world (this character's discovery during her interior dialogue is similar to Quiela's self-discoveries through her letter-writing in *Dear Diego*). As Janet Gold has discussed, this woman's inner being proves not to be empty or passively waiting to be filled, but rather the generator of images, the teller of tales, and a source of strength—a space where women may spend time with themselves. Thus the grasping of happiness is achieved by plunging into inner depths, rather than in the obtaining of a perfect lover or companion. Juan Bruce-Novoa (1996) considers this story principal among several of Poniatowska's stories that express a desire to be true to the individual search for happiness— happiness that can only be attained through freedom of action and spirit. Deborah Shaw sees the story as turning the tables, denouncing the norms of traditionally constructed relationships, by exposing women's abnegation and the dominant role men have been allowed. Women's passivity—which is required in the discourse of romantic love—is seen as masochism and suffering. In this light, Poniatowska's stories written in the 1960s can be seen as feminist strategies before their time in her Mexican society.

Poniatowska's story from the 1970s is even more daring— less disguised in its analysis of the female role in society—and this main character has evolved from earlier questions and meditations posed by earlier characters. This character also employs parody in its critique of traditional women's roles. The story's overt message was hardly grasped by Mexican critics, however. "You Arrive by Nightfall" is a culminating vision of the woman who would revise her Mexican society. It was in the 1970s that Mexican women first made headway in the creation of their own roles, contrary to strict Catholic-cultural, and patriarchal, "traditional," requirements. Lilus can again be seen in the smiling and sweet-thinking Esmeralda, who does not judge any of her husbands for their ways, even the one who denounces her. When asked why she married them, she responds that she could never have had intimate relations without marriage, thus making a subtle point about the male code and social order that requires that women remain virgins until marriage. The story is an interesting reflection of male conduct in Mexican society, where tradition has permitted one legal wife and also lovers on the side. Poniatowska reverses this traditional cultural practice. As the judge attempts to explain and point out Esmeralda's wrongdoing, she seems not to comprehend his vulgar insinuations and even to disarm him with her subtle and innocent remarks. Here we can envision the young Poniatowska responding to a patriarchal society that would categorize her as a sweet-natured gossip-column writer or as the innocent author of unknowingly provocative children's texts.

In the short novel *Lilus Kikus* and in each of these stories, women characters espouse the traditional feminine qualities of waiting and hoping, caring for others, and remaining quiet. But these traits disguise a discourse of indifference to abuse and social inequalities, problematizing an adult woman character who sets her gaze on her society. Poniatowska's characters are curious, wanting always to grow and learn. They question over and over again, and they make requests, thus transcending the role that society has assigned them. Poniatowska's stories are not tales of entertainment but discourses of angst and growth, of sociopolitical commentary on her society. They are excellent early examples of postmodern elaboration where traditional plot is sacrificed to create thinking pieces on modern society. Since the 1980s, several Mexican women writers have deconstructed *official* history by inserting powerful women characters into their accounts. But it was Poniatowska's early fictional work that subtly created the first contemporary rebellious female subject.

Lilus Kikus has never been published in translation, and very few of Poniatowska's stories have appeared in anthologies. It is hoped that this book will inspire further reading of Poniatowska's work, and may serve as an introduction to a great writer's creative process and motivations. This rendering of Poniatowska's early fiction can provide insight into her later work currently in English translation. This, her first short novel, and subsequent short stories, demonstrate the original thinking and intelligence of a daring woman before there was a publication boom of women writers in late-twentieth-century Mexico. Elena Poniatowska's feminism was not recognized in her early publications because she purposefully disguised her feminist discourse in order to publish, but most likely also because her society did not wish to look any farther than the young writer's attractiveness. Poniatowska, with others before and during her generation, should be recognized for her powerful observations of a society where women have been second-class citizens in the hegemonic system.

Leonora Carrington

The artist of the illustrations included in the original publication of *Lilus Kikus* is considered an English painter in England, a surrealist in France, and a Mexican in Mexico. Leonora Carrington is currently celebrated internationally for both her painting and her novels, but in the 1950s in Mexico, she was becoming one of the best-known women artists in that country. Her first major one-person exhibition was held in Mexico City in 1957, and in

1962 she was commissioned to create a principal mural for the new National Museum of Anthropology in Mexico City. The enormous mural, titled *El mundo mágico de los mayas,* includes iconography from the *Popol Vuh,* with symbology indicating an evolved consciousness, and ancient sources illuminating the present generation's possibilities of *mestizo* identity. Carrington is a contemporary of the great muralists, of Frida Kahlo and many other women artists, many of whom have received little attention outside their country. Her artistic work seeks to reveal a past that is around and with us at all times. During her early years in Mexico, she researched both the cosmogony of ancient American indigenous peoples and the Hindu. Both Carrington's art and her novels explore the intricate web between the real and the visionary, the visible and the invisible.

Carrington is an immigrant who arrived in Mexico the same year as Poniatowska, 1942, although she was some sixteen years older. She was born in 1917 to a wealthy British family (her mother was Irish) who had trouble understanding their gifted child. She was sent to an Italian boarding school at age fifteen, where her imaginative nature and artistic ambitions were encouraged. She returned to England at the height of European Modernism and studied with Amedée Ozenfant, through whom she met the German painter and sculptor Max Ernst. They left to reside in Paris, where in 1938 she participated in the International Surrealist Exhibition with such artists as Marcel Duchamp and André Breton.

Upon the outbreak of war in 1939, Ernst was placed in a concentration camp. Carrington fled for her life to Spain, where she suffered a nervous collapse and was institutionalized and declared insane. After several months, her family was able to get her released from the institution and planned to take her to South Africa. She escaped from them, however, and sought refuge at the Mexican consulate in Madrid where Mexican diplomat Renato Leduc arranged a marriage with her in order to get her safely out of Europe. They arrived in New York City in 1941, where Ernst had also just arrived, in the company of art collector Peggy Guggenheim. Carrington showed her work in surrealist exhibitions and wrote for artistic literary reviews until the following year, when she and Leduc moved to Mexico City. The couple dissolved their union, and Carrington soon married Hungarian refugee and photographer Erico "Chiki" Weisz; they raised two sons and Mexico became her permanent home. Her associations with Ernst and Leduc immersed her in the world of European surrealism, but a tendency toward a mythic quality in her work intensified in Mexico. Although it is uncertain whether Carrington would call herself a surrealist, she was associated with a group of surrealists (many of whom were Europeans who had migrated to Mexico), which included Remedios Varos, Wolfgang Paalen, and Luis Buñuel.

The 1940s and 1950s in Mexico were a fascinating era: ancient indigenous sites were being discovered and studied for the first time since the Spanish conquest, and strong support existed for cultural and artistic activities. Carrington moved in social circles where visits were made to pyramids and temples as they opened to the public. Although influenced by such artists as Bosch and Brueghel as well as the pre-war surrealist movement, Carrington's early exposure to Irish folktales and legends also influenced her creative work in Mexico. Celtic belief in the existence of another world that mirrors the world of everyday life is surprisingly similar to Mexican indigenous beliefs in relationships between the living and the dead.

While she continued to paint, by the 1970s Carrington also began to publish novels, which she wrote in English. Her highly acclaimed *The Hearing Trumpet* features the triumph of unaggressive and spontaneous female principle over the ruthless, hierarchical, and unimaginative male spirit. Carrington is credited with leadership in launching the women's liberation movement in Mexico in the early 1970s; she once stated that if women remained passive, there would be little hope of survival on earth. Because of her work on feminist issues, it is understandable that the young Poniatowska would have sought Carrington's depictions for her short novel.

Each of the drawings that accompany the chapters in *Lilus Kikus* expresses a subjective, interiorized vision of the child character's contemplations on life. Carrington made a gift to Poniatowska of these drawings, which were sketched upon reading the young author's narrative. They have not been exhibited elsewhere, and Poniatowska gave the framed originals to her daughter, Paula. They presently hang in her home in Mérida, Yucatán. Carrington still lives in Mexico City, but travels frequently to the United States—one of her sons lives in Chicago— and Europe.

Elizabeth Coonrod Martínez
January 2004

BIBLIOGRAPHY

Agosín, Marjorie. *A Woman's Gaze: Latin American Women Artists.* Fredonia, N.Y.: White Pine Press, 1998.

Bruce-Novoa, Juan. "Elena Poniatowska: The Feminist Origins of Commitment." *Women's Studies International Forum* 6:5 (1983): 309–516.

———. "Los cuentos de Elena Poniatowska." *El cuento mexicano: Homenaje a Luis Leal.* Edited by Sara Poot Herrera. México: Difusión Cultural, Serie El Estudio, 1996.

Camacho de Schmidt, Aurora. "Elogio del asombro: Cincuenta años de trabajo periodístico y literario de Elena Poniatowska." Unpublished paper delivered as opening presentation for Special International Colloquium honoring Elena Poniatowska at El Colegio de Mexico, Mexico City, September 24–26, 2003.

Flori, Monica. "Visions of Women: Symbolic Physical Portrayal as Social Commentary in the Short Fiction of Elena Poniatowska." *Third Woman* 2:2 (1984): 77–83.

García, Kay S. *Broken Bars: New Perspectives from Mexican Women Writers.* Albuquerque: University of New Mexico Press, 1999.

García Pinto, Magdalena. *Women Writers of Latin America: Intimate Histories.* Translated by Trudy Balch and Magdalena García Pinto. Austin: University of Texas Press, 1991.

Gold, Janet. "Feminine Space and the Discourse of Silence." *In the Feminine Mode: Essays on Hispanic Women Writers.* Edited by Noël Valis and Carol Maier. Lewisburg: Bucknell University Press, 1990.

Jorgensen, Beth. *The Writing of Elena Poniatowska: Engaging Dialogues.* Austin: University of Texas Press, 1994.

López González, Aralia. *Sin imágenes falsas, sin falsos espejos: Narradoras mexicanas del siglo XX.* México: El Colegio de México, 1995.

Martínez, Elizabeth Coonrod. "Avant-Garde Mexican Women Artists." *Hispanic Outlook in Higher Education* (February 25, 2002): 20–22.

————. Book Review of *La piel del cielo*. *Hispania* 86:4 (December 2003).

————. Book Review of *Paseo de la Reforma*. *Hispania* 82:2 (May 1999).

Moorhead, Florencia. "Subversion with a Smile: Elena Poniatowska's 'The Night Visitor.'" *Letras femeninas* (Boulder, Colo.) 20:1–2 (1994): 131–40.

Orenstein, Gloria Feman. "Hermeticism and Surrealism in the Visual Works of Leonora Carrington as a Model for Latin-American Symbology." In *Comparative Poetics: Proceedings of the 10th Congress of International Comparative Literature Association*. Edited by James W. Wilhelm, et al. New York: Garland, 1988.

Peden, Margaret Sayers. *Out of the Volcano: Portraits of Contemporary Mexican Artists*. Washington, D.C.: Smithsonian Institution Press, 1991

Poniatowska, Elena. "Escritoras chicanas y mexicanas." *La Jornada* (28 June 1993): 25–26.

————. *Lilus Kikus*. México: Ediciones Era, 1954.

————. *Los cuentos de Lilus Kikus*. Xalapa, Mexico: Universidad Veracruzana, 1967.

————. *Hasta no verte, Jesús mío*. México: Ediciones Era, 1969.

————. *La noche de Tlatelolco*. México: Ediciones Era, 1971.

————. *Querido Diego, te abraza Quiela*. México: Biblioteca Era, 1978.

————. *De noche vienes*. Mexico: Editorial Grijalbo, 1979; Ediciones Era, 1991.

————. *Gaby Brimmer*. México: Editorial Grijalbo, 1979.

————. *Fuerte es el silencio*. México: Ediciones Era, 1980.

————. *Nada, nadie: Las voces del temblor*. México: Ediciones Era, 1988.

————. *Tinísima*. México: Biblioteca Era, 1992.

————. *Luz, luna y las lunitas*. México: Ediciones Era, 1994.

————. *Paseo de la reforma*. México: Plaza y Janés, 1996.

————. *Las siete cabritas*. México: Ediciones Era, 2000.

————. *Las mil y una . . . (la herida de Paulina)*. Barcelona: Plaza y Janés, 2000.

———. *La piel del cielo*. Santiago de Chile: Alfaguara, 2001.

———. *Tlapalería*. México: Ediciones Era, 2003.

Poot Herrera, Sara. "Del Tornasol de *Lilus Kikus* al Tornaviaje de *La flor de Lis*." *Escribir la infancia: Narradoras mexicanas contemporáneas*. Edited by Nora Pasternac, et al. Pp. 59–80. Mexico: El Colegio de México, 1996.

Richards, Katharine. "A Note on Contrasts in Elena Poniatowska's 'De noche vienes.'" *Letras Femeninas* (Lincoln, Nebr.) 70:1–2 (1991): 107–11.

Shaw, Deborah. "Gender and Class Relations in 'De noche vienes' by Elena Poniatowska." *Bulletin of Hispanic Studies* (Glasgow, Scotland) 72:1 (Jan. 1995): 111–21.

Vargas, Margarita. "Power and Resistance in 'De noche vienes' by Elena Poniatowska." *Hispanic Journal* 16:2 (fall 1995): 285–96.

Elena Poniatowska's Works in Translation

Dear Diego. Translated by Katherine Silver. New York: Pantheon Books, 1986.

Massacre in Mexico. Translated by Helen R. Lane. Columbia: University of Missouri Press, 1992.

Nothing, Nobody: The Voices of the Mexico City Earthquake. Translated by Aurora Camacho de Schmidt. Philadelphia: Temple University Press, 1995.

Tinísima. Translated by Katherine Silver. Penguin, 1998.

Here's to you, Jesusa! Translated by Deanna Heikkinen. New York: Farrar, Straus & Giroux, 2001.

The Skin of the Sky. Translated by Deanna Heikkinen. New York: Farrar, Straus & Giroux, 2004.

"Love Story." Translated by Beth Miller. *Latin American Literary Review* 13:26 (1985): 65–73.

"Slide in My Dark One, Between the Crosstie and the Whistle." Translated by Cynthia Steele. In *Beyond the Border: A New Age in Latin American Women's Fiction*. Edited by Nora Erro-Peralta and Caridad Silva-Núñez. Pp. 125–43. Pittsburgh, Pa.: Cleis Press, 1991.

PART 1

THE SHORT NOVEL
Lilus Kikus

Lilus's Toys and Distractions

"Lilus Kikus . . . Lilus Kikus . . . Lilus Kikus, I am calling you!"

But Lilus Kikus, seated on the sidewalk near the street, was much too absorbed in her manipulation of a fly to hear her mother's screams. Lilus never plays in her room, that room that has lost all sense of order. She would rather play on the street corner, beneath a small tree planted at the edge of the sidewalk. From her vantage point, she can watch cars go by, and people who walk very quickly, with faces set like they're going to save the world.

Lilus believes in witches and sews into her britches a little sprig of fine herbs, rosemary and grass; and a hair of Napoleon, one of those they sell outside the school for 10 cents. And also her tooth, the first one to come out. All of these she put into a little bag that now rests over her navel. The other girls would later ask at school what causes that little bulge in front of her belly. In a small box, Lilus also keeps the black ribbon from a dead person's casket; two small, gray, and hard pieces of her father's toenails; a three-leaf clover; and the dust collected near the feet of a statue of Christ in the church of Our Lady of Piety.

When she visited her uncle's ranch, Lilus discovered her own toys and games. She had a bird's nest, which she spent hours and hours contemplating, observing the little eggs' fragility. She followed step by step, with great interest, all the mother bird's doings: "Now sleep . . . after a while she will go find some food," she whispered softly to the eggs. She also has a centipede, saved in a sock, and some huge flies that received operations on their appendages. At the ranch there are also ants, some very fat ants. Lilus gave them syrup for a cough, and plastered their fractured legs. One day she searched in the village pharmacy for a syringe with a very fine needle, in order to provide an emergency injection to Miss Lemon. Miss Lemon was a fat green lime that suffered from scary abdominal pains, and that Lilus injected regularly with black coffee. Afterward, she wrapped Miss Lemon in one of her mother's handkerchiefs, and in the afternoon she waited on other patients: Mrs. Orange, Eva the apple, the widow Grapefruit, and the Honorable Mr. Banana. Bitter over the vicissitudes of this life, Mr. Banana suffered from military gout, and, since he was not as strong as the other patients, he would soon see the end of his days.

Lilus Kikus does not have any dolls. Perhaps her physique explains why. She is skinny and takes large steps as she walks, because her legs—long and very separated one from the other—are jumpy; she trips and gets them tangled together if she does not take large steps. When Lilus falls, it causes the inevitable death of a doll. That is why she never has any dolls. She only remembers one little golden-haired doll that she named Blondie Punch, who expired the next day after her arrival in this world, when Lilus's feet got tangled up and she tripped.

The Concert

One day Lilus's mother decided to take her to a concert at the Palace of Fine Arts. It was a mass of a building, white with a little gold trim, and somewhat sunken.

Lilus has three record albums that she plays at all hours. When she feels a little theatrical, she cries and laughs to the tempo of the music. Even during *The Passion According to St. Matthew*, she found a way to grimace, smile, and pull her hair. She undid her braids, and threw herself onto the bed, fanning herself with a cardboard and pretend-smoking her father's oriental pipe. Lilus's reading habits are never supervised, and one day she fell upon this paragraph: "Nothing better expresses man's feelings, his passions, anger, sweetness, ingenuity, or sadness, than music. You will find in music the conflicts of your own heart. It's a crash between desires and needs, the desire of purity and the need to know." So now when her mother announced that she would take her to the concert, Lilus put on the face of an explorer, and off the two went.

A poor little man slept during the concert. A short, hapless man with even breathing. He slept sadly, with his head to one side, restless for having fallen asleep. As the violin stopped playing, his sleep was interrupted, and the man raised his head slightly; but as the violin picked up again, his head once again fell onto his shoulder. Then the snores covered the violin sounds.

This irritated people. Some young women laughed quietly. The older people absorbed themselves in the music, apparently not able to hear anything else. But one couple— man and woman (the type who are concerned for the welfare of humanity)—sporadically, quickly and discreetly, gave him little slaps on the back.

And the poor little man kept right on sleeping. He was sad and stupid. Stupid because it is horrible to sleep among the waking. Sad because maybe in his house the bed was too narrow, and his wife in it too fat. And the overstuffed chair, which served as his seat at the Fine Arts Palace, must have seemed extremely comfortable.

Often people cry because they find things just too beautiful. What makes them cry is not the desire to possess those things, but that profound melancholy that we all feel for what isn't, and for all that doesn't reach its fullness. It is the sadness of the dry riverbed, that little path that writhes without water, the tunnel under construction and never finished, and the pretty faces with stained teeth. That is the sadness of all that is not complete.

Lilus the explorer dedicates her time to watching the spectators. There are some who quietly concentrate on the orchestra, seemingly suffering as though the musicians might miss a note at any moment. They set their faces as great connoisseurs, and with one gesture of the hand, or a low murmur of a known phrase, they make their neighbors aware of their

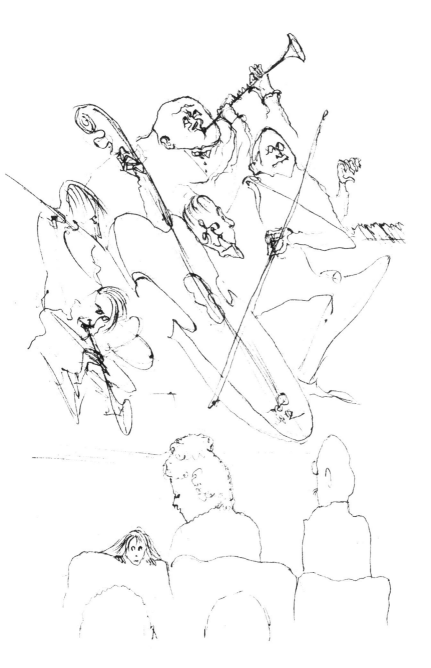

great musical knowledge. Others listen with more humility. Ashamed, they don't know what to do with their hands. They wait eagerly for each applause period; they watch, hardly breathing, and are mortified each time a stranger chooses to blow his nose, cough, or applaud at the wrong time. These are the innocents who participate in everyone's blame. The others are very conscious of their humanity, worried over a minor gesture, the program, or a wrinkle in their clothing. Once in a while someone gives himself over to his innermost impulses. With a look of ecstasy, eyes closed and nostrils very open, they deliver themselves to God knows what pleasures.

"Bravo! Bravísimo!" Amid the applause, and with a smiling face, Lilus's mother leans over to tell her: "The andante was marvelous. Oh, but my poor girl, you don't know what an andante is! Right away I am going to tell you the story of Mozart's life, and his andantes, and everything. . . ."

The two depart in happy spirits. Lilus because she believes she is going to hear a story. Her mother, because she's convinced she's an intellectual.

T H R E E

Lilus in Acapulco

Sun! Sun! Sun! There's nothing more than sun, sand, and sea. The sea! At night you hear the noise it makes, and in the morning you see it sparkling against the beach. At night it disturbs Lilus. She feels bothered by a black, almost evil sea, and she thinks about the wind that seems to punish the sea unceasingly.

Lilus walks everywhere on her long legs, with her eyes open wide at all times, constantly afraid of missing something. She has become nervous, restless, and whimsical. The sea bewilders her. Now Lilus is a child of the sea, of sand, of brine, of salt, and wind. She is a girl of seashells and conches, of great waves of water that hit her face like bursts of rain.

Lilus is all golden and nicely browned like a loaf of bread just out of the oven. She's not one of those girls who go to the beach with shovels, towels, pails, molds, and suits to change into, who spoil the marine view with all of their assorted equipment to pamper themselves. Lilus entertains herself with what she discovers on the beach: shells, starfish, water, and sand. And with those things that the sea leaves at its edge, things that seem so beautiful, and that are seldom any more than a piece of wood spit out by the waves.

Lilus walks with one foot in the water and one foot on the dry sand. In the city she also walked that way—one foot on the curb and the other on the pavement. That is why she always walks a little off balance. While she sways so, Lilus dreams, and it soothes her to walk this way like a boat.

She dreams that she owns a castle, called The Distant Castilian. For the first time she thinks of men; there are many on the beach. Some skinny like rats with tight swimsuits. Others fat and red, shiny from oil. She doesn't like them. They seem like great red fish, in their scandalous nudity. They remind her of *The Romans in their Decadence*, an oil painting of a butchery she saw in a museum. Lilus dreams that she is walking with Ivar's dogs. Ivar is her husband. She walks barefoot and hears the noise the sand makes as it crunches beneath her feet. She is alone and has a strong desire to throw herself onto the beach, or to jump very high and indecorously between the waves. She simply cannot resist. If her husband finds out, he will say she should be more serious and more dignified (he's a little functionary), and perhaps he threatens her with locking her in a convent. But she won't let him finish his scolding; she'll throw her arms of water and salt around his neck; she will show him her necklaces of small, blue shells, so tender they resemble children's eyelids as they sleep, and of hard shells that look like the teeth of killer fish. Or she'll tell him God has made nature not only to look upon but also so that we may live in her, and that each person has his own wave, and won't he please choose his. And that from the heavens, God is watching his children swimming in the sea, just as a mother duck watches her ducklings. And he will say . . . , and she will leave him without a breath of protest. . . .

Lilus awakens. Some guys just hollered at her, "Oh, b-a-b-y, wish I were a train to make a stop on your curves!" This makes her think, "What curves?" The part about "baby" doesn't bother her; after all, she's not the guy's child.

Lilus walks contentedly, swinging her tail. What triumph, her by the sea! What sun on the water! What water against the sky! What sand in the heat! What a flutter of white wings in the air! She can't even think anymore; she prefers to sing. But the only song that occurs to her is the Caribbean song *Cafetal*:

> *Because people live criticizing me,*
> *I spend my life thinking of nothing...*

Lilus feels pretty. She throws herself on the sand, alone and stretching out her arms, pregnant with the sea, looking anxiously at waves that rise and bow down far from her, lifting their huge heads as though they would swallow her in a great lion's mouth.

F O U R

Political Elections

Lilus goes into downtown Acapulco. She brought shells from the sea and has some currency, bills of a thousand colors. She will make a necklace. She is going to buy a long thread to string the shells. She will put it around her neck, or around the waist, or knit it into her braids, tied at the ends to a stone.... But instead she encounters a rally.

"Hey! Why don't they keep the same president and that way stay out of trouble? But no." This is a demonstration by many Seven Machos party members, and they are screaming: "The will of the people . . . the future of Mexico . . . our natural resources . . . our welfare." And Lilus thinks about the people. Which ones are they? The people are selling lottery tickets in English, over there by Madero and San Juan de Letrán streets; buying whisky in the Doctors neighborhood; and lighting candles in the Guadalupe district. Lilus is not very patriotic, and she knows it. At school there are those who post propaganda, and others who take it down. And because of that, it is considered

meritorious to participate in these acts. Lilus limited herself to asking one classmate how they made the notices stick, and he replied: "With my tongue, stupid." At night, Lilus dreamed, repentantly, that she had a huge pink tongue, and that she used it to apply massive posters. The next morning she awoke with her mouth open and her tongue dry.

Lilus presses through the crowd and between the Seven Machos members. Some listen with a face of "We will save Mexico!" They sweat profusely. They are men of strong will. Others are just standing there to see what will happen. After a while, they pull out their Pepín comics, and get into "Rose, the Seductress." They are men of divided will. There are also some women. Some are fat, others skinny; they also know a lot about law, that is, of farm hands, of refugees, and of the Jackal of Peralvillo. They talk among themselves, commenting, "Oh what a horrible horror! Look, Mrs. Rurris, at these men who are such monkeys. What one does, another follows. Last night I noticed a jackal face on my husband." "Oh Felipa, how barbarous!" In regard to the refugees, their decision was that they should go back to the States, because here they make too much of themselves.

Suddenly, a wave of pressure splits the demonstration between the strong-willed men and the divided-will men. Everyone starts talking much louder. There are a few shouts, and it occurs to Lilus to also shout: "Long live Mr. Cástulo Rat!" And, boom ba boom! Some of the Seven Machos lift Lilus off the ground, a stiff but patriotic Lilus Kikus.

During the tumult, police arrive, and an hour later the police take down Lilus's declaration, and she answers meekly with a trembling voice: "Well, having seen that those at my school had done so many things, I thought that the least I could do was add a little yell."

Lilus tramps home, and along the way it occurs to her that if they had roughed her up a little harder, she might have ended up in the hospital. Mr. Cástulo Rat might then have gone to visit her in a black car to offer her the "Virtuous Lilus Kikus" medal. The newspaper would publish her picture with the words: "Lilus Kikus seduces the people." And on the Society page: "The gorgeous Lilus Kikus, wearing a lovely dress, defended unspeakable horrors against her party. It is obvious she loves her party humongously." But even that does not lift her spirits.

Lilus is disillusioned. Things always happen to her only halfway.

Nothing to Do . . .

Lilus awakens with the sun. Since there are no curtains in her wide bedroom, the sun enters without notice and cracks like a whip across her pillow. Lilus would like to possess one of those rays, to touch it and let it slide through her fingers. How funny it would be to have fingernails of sunlight! At night she could read from the light of her nails, the light of the sparks projected from her fingertips. When she would wash her hands (which does not happen regularly) she would take care not to wet her fingertips too much. When playing the piano, she would have a little lantern for each note. While combing her hair, sprinkles of light would shine through her hair. Maybe they would even take her to the circus as a phenomenon to place between the bearded lady and the fat woman.

Today she has nothing to do. How wonderful! When Lilus has nothing to do, she doesn't do anything. She sits on the last step of the staircase, and remains there while Aurelia cleans. The windows are opened wide, and the sun pours in, trapping the dust in

each ray. Giant spirals of gray gold. Lilus shakes the stars of dust with her hands, but the sun defends them and they return docilely to occupy their same place in the spiral. There they continue spinning and heating themselves in the rays of light.

Lilus talks to Aurelia the maid and asks her: "What kind of kisses does your boyfriend give you?"

"Puckered kisses, little one, puckered kisses." Lilus is transfixed thinking about what the puckered kisses might be like.

Lilus's father doesn't like to see her doing nothing. "Go get some exercise. Run! You're going to become a witch if you just keep sitting there looking at who-knows-what." Lilus's father doesn't understand her when she remains still and watching a kitten play with its tail, or a drop of dew slowly slide from a leaf for entire hours. Lilus knows why the rocks want to be alone. She knows when it is going to rain, because the sky is without horizon, compassionate. She has held in her hands warm birds and has placed cold feathers in their nests. She is transparent and cheerful. One day she captured a lightning bug and spent all night with it, asking how it enclosed the light. She has walked barefoot over the cold grass and over moss, jumping, laughing, and singing out of sheer happiness. Lilus's father never walks barefoot. He has too many appointments. He constructs his life like a house, with numerous rooms full of acts and decisions. He makes a schedule for each day, and pretends to hold Lilus within a very rigid order. Lilus feels anguished.

Heaven

Lilus is worried about how to get into heaven. She is no heretic. She knows that heaven is a state of mind, a manner of being, and not a place, and. . . . Always, and since she was little, however, she has thought that Our Father was way up high above the clouds. Up there. And in order to get there, to be able to reach Him, one has to be a plane, an angel, or a bird. While the bird-Lilus would be rising through the heavens, God would be looking at her. And at some juncture in her/its flight, God's look would be so intense as to convert her into a golden dove, more beautiful than an angel.

Since the day of her First Communion, Lilus has thought that Our Father would send His Spirit down in a little elevator installed in her throat. Our Father would take that elevator to come down to Lilus's soul and would stay there in a special room of His choice. So that He would enjoy visiting, she needed to prepare a well-furnished room. Lilus's sacrifices became the furnishings. A huge sacrifice became the sofa, another the bed.

The small sacrifices were simply chairs, vases of flowers, decorations, or side tables.

One week when Lilus let herself go completely, Our Father came down to the room of her soul and found it completely empty. He had to sit on the bare floor, even lie down to sleep on the bare floor.

But just as you become impregnated by someone, even after that someone is gone, that is how Lilus remained, full of Our Father, who had come down to her soul in a little elevator.

The Religious Procession

"Girls, quickly, everyone in line for the procession."

"Yes, Miss. Uh-oh, the Lamb's not here!"

"Where is that child? Well, one of Mary's Daughters may go look for her. Look, Martha, your veil is all crooked and your slip is showing."

Some two hundred girls dressed in white, with large tulle veils, are preparing for a procession in honor of the Virgin Mary. They pinch their legs, they put on and take off their white gloves, and they keep feverishly passing a fragile crepe-paper lily from one hand to the other.

"Let's see, girls, let us practice. Everyone repeat after me: 'Oh Mother, I offer you the lily of my heart. It is yours for all of life.'"

"Oh Mother, I offer you the lily of my heart. It is yours for all of life."

"Lilus! What is that you're saying under your breath? Say it right now out loud and in front of the entire school!"

"Well, I just said that white looks very bad on Martha and that her veil . . . "

"Lilus! You will write eighty times, 'I should not be uncharitably criticizing my schoolmates.' And let's see, Mary's Daughters, where is the Lamb?"

"Miss, we haven't seen her anywhere."

"Well, we can't wait for her any longer. The moment has come to begin our journey toward the image. Don't forget your reverence; please, say it in the most gracious way possible—before kneeling in front of the Most Holy Virgin—and very carefully leave your lily in the baskets set up for them."

"Miss?"

"What is it, Martha?"

"I know where the Lamb is. I saw her about ten minutes ago, but I didn't want to tell on her. . . . "

"Tell on her about what?"

"That she was dipping her lily in an inkstand."

"What? In an inkstand?"

"Yes. And in one with black ink."

"What a girl! My goodness! I'll have to speak with the Mother Superior. But we can't lose any more time. Come along, girls, march. Everyone in the same tempo. One two, one two, one two."

Slowly the chaotic procession of elves in transparent whiteness moves forward. Flighty muslins, tulles stiff above the heads, and white, shiny shoes. Little faces set nervously for a great ceremony. "One two, one two, one two." Lilus walks next to Martha, and Martha doesn't know how to keep step. With reason—she has feet like boats. In order to reach the image, they must simply cross three long halls and two dormitories. And suddenly, as they reach the first dormitory, now marching with rhythmic pace, the Lamb appears! The very cross-eyed, more cross-eyed than ever Lamb, with a supremely wrinkled dress and terrible veil.

Lilus Kikus 55

"Lamb, how atrocious!"

The Lamb is aloof during the rest of the procession, and in a general stupor, marches a diabolical dance—a cross between the Charleston and can-can. She makes the gestures of a scarecrow, and swings a sullied lily. The unforeseen macabre dance is accompanied by the following words from her lips, in a high-pitched tone:

"So what?
I'm not a virgin.
Zambumba Mother the Rumba.
My black and blue lily . . .
Zambumba Mother what a zumba.
So what?"

Later, before the statue, the girls try to make the Most Holy Virgin forget this shameful incident, and declare in their sweetest voices: "Oh Mother, I offer the lily of my heart . . ."

The Black Sheep

"Lilus? Lilus!"

"Yes, Lamb?"

"Come help me pack my bag."

"Did you see the Mother Superior?"

"Yes, stupid. And tomorrow I am going home."

"What did she say to you?"

"Only insults. Among others, that I was 'the black sheep in this most white flock.'"

"Oh gosh! I am going to miss you, Lamb."

"Well of course. Since you will no longer have someone to ask why your skirts fasten on the side and not in front, with three little gray buttons, like the boys."

"Oh, Lamb! I have never asked you that. It has never even occurred to me . . ."

"Well, it's about time it occurred to you. You and that group of stupid girls who receive instruction here are not taught well."

"Pretty little Lamb, really, teach me. Tell me the story."

"Listen to me, 'cause it's not a story. Look, Lilus, I know so many things, that right now I could tell you how babies are born through the navel. And many other things, but you are such a ninny you wouldn't understand anything. And besides, you never give me anything for the things that I tell you."

"Some chocolate crèmes, would you like? But tell me about those buttons. Come on, tell me, little Lamb."

"Chocolates, no. They'd be ruined during my trip."

"Some sharp, very pointed, colored pencils?"

"No. I'm in a hurry. Pass me my shirts so I can put them in the suitcase."

"Lamb, if you don't tell me, I'll writhe in desperation. Word of honor!"

"Well, writhe all you want. Look, Lilus, maybe for the chocolates, it wouldn't be entirely impossible for me to tell you about my first love. But only about my first love."

"Oh, heavenly Lamb! Tell me."

"Grownups think that you can't suffer heartbreak when you're thirteen years old. But yes, you can, and that pain is hidden because of timidity, and the great torment is endured silently. It torments you to know you were misunderstood, to not have risked yourself, and to wait. It torments you to hear during introductions, in front of your family's old friends, these words on your mother's lips: 'Here is my daughter, Laura Lamb. She was so cute last year, but now she's at that awkward age, you know, when they're neither girls nor women.'

"And I, Laura Lamb, who was full of noble and suffering thoughts, rebelled against such injustice.

"Early loves are the ones that watch you on the street corners, and then go away to dream. They're loves you cannot touch, but which evoke a lot. When I was thirteen, I fell in love. I was content just to look at him from afar, never to speak to him. At night I would always fall asleep thinking of him. I didn't hope to be held in his arms, or anything. My lack of curiosity was complete."

"But now?"

"Now I am completely disillusioned with love, Lilus. Now I only think of maternity, and I have taken steps toward. . . . "

And so the Lamb was expelled. She left with a Scottish bag in her hand, and huge, dark glasses upon her face like prosthetic tears. She stuck her tongue out at the director, and she gave Lilus two stupendous grimaces, and promised her that she would soon send her a bottle of champagne.

Illness

Lilus shivers between the two humid sheets. She doesn't know why she's sick. The illness surged without warning, traitorous, like a great wave of solitude. Health is an easily lost object: "But I had it in my hand, only a little while ago I saw it." That is how her illness was: "But only yesterday I was running on the stairway."

Lilus's illness wasn't a cold, nor the flu, nor a stomach ache. She tended to fall ill over something said to her. Upon hearing something unexpected, she became afraid. She wouldn't turn to anyone, nor did she want to be babied. Secretly, she embraced her illness. She'd let herself be invaded by the feeling, and it would seem that the whole world penetrated her being. Her mother, her father, Aurelia, Ocotlana ...Lilus loved them even more, seeing in them the emissaries of her illness. These people pressed about above her and gave form to her illness, a clearly defined form. Happily, Lilus closed herself off within the borders of her illness.

"Oh, Lord Jesus, Lord Jesus, I don't feel my feet. I think I have one of them in one eye, a hand in my throat, and my

stomach—could it be the pillow?" The doctor was tardy in arriving with his instruments. Lilus saw figures appear and disappear in the haze above her. Huge red figures asked things of some green dwarfs and then dissolved into decomposed forms. Frogs and toads leaped about the room. They would slide when they hit the sheets, and Lilus stretched out a hand, trying to reach them. But they would always slip and slide away. "Oh, Lord Jesus, why did you go to the wedding of Cana, to that party of drunks? Why did you perform that odd miracle?"

"Little Lilus, Jesus wasn't rigorous, and those good people needed to have some fun. They had no wine, and needed wine for the party."

"Mother, I want some wine, some red wine!"

"Precious little Lilus, don't be silly."

"But I am at a wedding party, Mother. . . . "

In dreams, Lilus drinks happily, feverishly. "Jesus, at the wedding of Cana. And the adulteress? What must you do to become an adulteress?"

Lilus saw Mary Magdalene open her perfume decanters. . . .

Through the fog of her illness, Lilus sees many women pass, stiff and moralistic, with black letters on their chests and backs that say, "Prohibited, Prohibited," and who threaten her with expulsion from the organization Flowering Souls. Lilus feels enclosed and imprisoned. Intentions float out of a file, and Lilus hears an old, skinny woman tell her: "We save without charging, we'll save you even if you don't want to be saved. But don't cross another word with those of 'Immediate Pardon,' because they are irresponsible and for advertising only."

"But lady, I am not lost. I only came for a little while to the wedding of Cana, which is a very happy party where people are well behaved."

"You are a gluttonous virgin, Lilus, and you always only go

halfway. You don't even have the courage to really lose yourself, so that your salvation would be worth it. You don't give in, and you stand on the edge, watching calmly as others drown. Your mother doesn't realize this, and thinks you're a little ray of sunshine, an angel with no apparent wings. Take the scapular!"

The scapular is made of a very rough cloth, and hurts her chest and back, like sticky sand. Lilus is troubled by the woman of sworn virtue who says such strange things. "I don't understand you, you skinny old lady." Lilus feels dizzy. Now she's riding on a boat and is afraid of falling into the water. "It's your lifesaver, you wicked little girl." That's what the gaunt old lady says as she places the scapular on Lilus. The boat reels. A doctor with the face of a devil sits on the edge of the bed.

"Doctor, this child has a very high fever. I don't know what to do."

"'Tis true, madam, 'tis true. What is your daughter's name?"

"Lilus Kikus."

"Lulis Pikus, what a pretty name. I'll take care of her; she's going to get well right away. This prescription will get her temperature down."

And the doctor takes Lilus's pulse with his hairy hand. Then he writes a list of interminable mortal sins on his prescription tablet. With childlike eyes, unknowing and wanting to know everything, Lilus's mother is transfixed, watching the doctor.

"Madam, don't you worry a bit. I am going to take care of her, from this day on; I will be the angel who guards your daughter, Pilus Liki . . . "

"Lilus Kikus, doctor."

"Pardon me, I don't have a good memory for names, but I am going to put things in order for Kilus Lukis."

And the devil puts away his instruments and starts laughing. "What is my name? Where am I and who am I?" The people look at Lilus with an air of complicity and cynicism. "Oh yes, I'm Kolis Liko, Kukis Piki, Fuchis Lokis, and I am sailing on the boat of fever." The passengers have glassy, sweet eyes. They walk like seals, slowly, heavy and humid. Lilus tries to pick up an object, to satiate herself in her reality, squeezing it with her hands, but her hands are two dead fish that do not obey her. "It's twelve o'clock," someone says. And twelve concentric circles form in the water. Lilus runs through doors and hallways, while someone chases her. She loses a shoe on a stairway, but continues fleeing, limping. "Holy God, Sainted Strength, Saint Immortal, have pity on me. . . . " Suddenly the boat's deck ends, and one Lilus Kikus of lead plunges to the bottom of the sea, heavy with secrets.

"Mother! Mother! Mother, I am drowning!"

"Hush, child, finally you were sleeping."

"It's because I haven't told you so many things, Mother. Mother, Mommy, oh Mommy, I am so guilty. Go call the man at number four, he didn't go to the wedding of Cana, and he'll be angry when he knows I went. He never goes to parties, and there was a lovely wine there. I also wanted to show him my little doll, the one I got out of the Three Kings cake."

"What things are you saying?"

"The man at number four, Mother, please send for him."

"When you get well, Lilus, when you get well, my little baby. Look, your fever's already gone down. I'll open the window for you."

The Dividing Wall

"Child, come down from the wall."

"No."

"I am telling you to come down."

"I said no."

"Pretty little girls don't climb..."

"Leave me..."

"I am going to tell your mother."

"She won't do anything to me anyway." Ocotlana runs toward the house.

"Go on, you old tattletale, dirty mush." The lizard? Where did the lizard go? That dummy Ocotlana scared it. Ocotlana! Each time she speaks, a little bit of saliva comes out of the corner of her mouth. Her stockings get stuck with a kind of knot that forms just behind her knees. When she climbs on a bus, her white and limp skin shakes between her stockings and her skirt. "Oh, lizard! Where are you? Lovely pink lizard, I brought you a little handkerchief."

Lilus climbs up on the dividing wall regularly. She climbs it because from there she can see into the window of a very strange man who lives in the apartment building next door. The man is forever sitting in front of a worktable, and he thumbs through great quantities of old books. The first day Lilus saw him she continued to watch him for about an hour. She watched him read and reread without moving, like a wizard before his crystal ball. Then he stood up and he put things and more things in their places in the air, in invisible categories and compartments, with his two rapid and almost transparent hands.

Since then Lilus has returned every day to her observation post, to spy on such incomprehensible activity. Until today, when she could not bear it any longer, and she began to howl from her wall: "Oh, Mister, from apartment number four! Mr. from number fo-o-o-ur!" Since she didn't get a response, she gathered a fistful of pebbles, and began to throw them, one by one, against the windowpane. But nothing. The man in number four would not move. He had his head deeply involved in a great book with red binding. He must have thought it was hailing, and without realizing it, included Lilus in his analysis of meteor showers.

Completely exasperated, Lilus decided that the only solution was to yell for help, while increasing the caliber of her projectiles. Could he be deaf and dumb? "Mr. from number fo-o-o-ur! Help! S.O.S.!" And oh, surprise of surprises, when one of Lilus's stones was about to break the window, the man from number four slowly turned his head, lifted his gaze from the books, and brought it to rest on Lilus.

"Mr. from number four...." (The man opens the bombarded window.) "Excuse me, Mr.-from-number-four, but is this your lizard?"

"No, child, the lizards don't belong to anyone."

"Well, since it is always in front of your window, I thought you put it out to sun itself."

And that was how the friendship between Lilus and the man from number four began. Three times a week at least, there would be Lilus on the adobe wall. The man would lose the flow of his readings as he opened the window and spoke to Lilus.

"Mr.-from-number-four, what things do you study? You're going to lose your mind. You look like a bird closed up in its cage. Why don't you go out for a walk?"

"I'm resolving antinomies. Last night I was stuck again on one of the Fragments, as though in an alley without an exit. No, it's not the one where 'new waters flow toward you,' but the other one. Also, non-Euclidean geometries. And then my students' texts are plagued with spiritual misprints. I spend my entire life correcting them."

"Mr.-from-number-four, do you remember the Lamb? The one I told you about the other day?"

"The lamb, the lamb . . . let me think. Ah yes, the feminist, the free thinker."

"Exactly. That one. Things went badly for her. They expelled her from school."

"Well, life started too early for her. You know, Lilus? I like talking to you. Mostly because I pull out of your conversation so many Alexandrine philosophies."

"What is that?"

"Also, you have made me become aware of the autumn. The moment in which everything is consumed. I had not taken notice since I was a child. I never examined the seasons. But what is wrong, Lilus? Today you don't talk as much as usual."

"It is because I am sad."

"About what?"

"That so many things happen to people."

"What things?"

"Well, those things that occur to you, like the theory of Pythagoras, the antinomies you told me about, and the non-Eudiclean geometries."

"Eudiclean, no, no. Euclidean, Lilus."

"Mr.-from-number-four, why don't you go out to the countryside? To the country, Mr.-from-number-four! Over there just above the foothills. As you walk along a little section I know, the trees are always more and more green and more shady, almost black, they are so close together. There's a spring there that only the birds know, and there are wild herbs and unkempt grass. No one makes noise. The silence is so great that you can hear the whispering of limbs and the humid movements of flowers. There you can make your moral geometries on the sand."

"Little girl, have pity on my struggle. Don't you know? These things have built up in me, they have devastated me and refined me. I am an expert in denunciations and experienced in misfortunes."

"Ah?"

"But sometimes you are right. I should ask forgiveness of so many things that are on the other side of my window. To the tree and to the plant, and if you wish, to the birds and the clouds."

"Yes, yes. You should ask forgiveness of the lizard that comes every day to take in the sun right alongside your window, and to some little clusters of sleeping flowers that you have never noticed. And above all, to the trees. It is so nice to stand beneath a tree looking at its green and full goblet, with large lakes of sky and clouds surrounding it. And you're so skinny. I'd like to know what you eat. And you have such sunken eyes. My mother is right now making some meringues. Would you like me to bring you one? Shall I jump down off the wall? Or should I use the ladder instead?"

"Lilus! L-i-l-u-s! Where are you? Once again up on the wall?"

"Oh, gosh, my mother!"

"Child! Come down immediately. You should be doing your homework!"

"I can't. My pen doesn't work. I used it to inject Ocotlana.

"What a child! Come down. Forgive her, sir, I don't know how you put up with her unceasing questions."

"Goodbye, goodbye, I'll see you tomorrow."

"Goodbye, little Lilus. Goodbye, madam."

As they walk, her mother scolds her. "Lilus, why do you take up that poor man's time? He's a philosopher, and you're up there just taking him away from his work. Lilus, my dear, when are you going to learn to discover your own answers to your infinity of questions?"

Lilus's Girlfriend

Lilus had a friend, Chiruelita. She was pampered and spoiled. At the age of eleven, Chiruela still spoke baby talk. When Lilus returned from Acapulco, her friend greeted her: "How it go? Didun the sharkies bite you, those uggy, bad fishees?"

Such a statement surprised Lilus, who had nearly forgotten her friend's way of talking. But she would soon get used to it again. All of her maternal instincts surged when she was with Chiruela, whom she dearly loved. Also, Lilus had heard it said that dummies are the most enchanting women in the world. That's right, those who know nothing, who are simply juvenile and absent, are the most alluring. Like the Latin figures, Ondina, Melisenda . . .

Of course, Chiruelita went a little overboard, but Lilus always forgave her, and she had all sorts of reasons and examples for her friend's behavior. After all, Goethe, who was so intelligent, had a wife who was like a fresh and innocent little girl, who knew nothing but was always happy.

No one ever said that the Holy Virgin knew Greek or Latin. The Virgin simply stretches out her arms, she opens them like a little child, and gives herself completely.

Lilus knows of the dangers that await those who attempt to speak well, and she would rather keep quiet. It is better to feel than to know. May beauty and grandeur come to us incognito, without the credentials we have memorized.

The women who listen and receive are like rivers swollen with rainwater; they deliver themselves as great waterfalls of happiness. This could seem an apology for dummies. But now that there are so many intellectual women, who teach, direct, and govern, it is so healthy and refreshing to suddenly discover a Chiruelita who speaks of flowers, frights, perfumes, and little strawberry tarts.

Chiruelita marries, at age seventeen, a languid and eccentric artist. He is a painter, and in the first few years he feels very happy with all of the curious occurrences and inconveniences of life with a simple and smiling woman. She serves him salted tea, and tells him every day the story of the little husband who got lost in bed, a story that always finishes in a wail each time more difficult to console.

But one day Chiruelita greets her husband with a crown of flowers in her hair and clasps of butterflies and cherries behind her ears, and whispers in her most melodious voice: "Hallo my widdle goat, me the Spwing of Botticelli. Today I make no sup fol you!" upon which, and with a languid gesture, the eccentric artist wrung her neck.

Convent School

"Lilus, you're going to . . . "

"You're going to go on a train."

"Trains are nice, aren't they, Lilus?"

"Your father and I are thinking of your future."

"Within a week you will be at the convent school."

A convent! A convent of nuns. Lilus had seen horrible nuns in her dreams. Faces of perfect insensitivity. Faces that no human problem could ever disturb. The immobility of a face is more terrifying than scars or blind eyes.

Lilus pictured the nuns as old women in black and with mustaches. Women with dry skin and pale tongues, who smelled like who-knows-what, very rancid and old. She imagined them praying sadly and mechanically, like a saw across a slab of wood, while Jesus in the heavens sweated desperately. She had heard them in the school dictating sententious maxims: "A treasure is not always a friend, but a friend is always a treasure," and "There are never roses without thorns nor thorns without roses."

How disgusting! Lilus thought, "Mother, I can't go to the convent school." Then, "Mommy! How do the nuns eat?" She saw them chewing the same piece of meat for hours—she, the one who can't stand seeing people eat slowly. On the other hand, Lilus is delighted with the Russians, who swallow an entire canapé of caviar at once.

It occurred to her that the nuns would not let her go outdoors, that she would no longer feel the cold grass under her feet, nor play in the green, white, and blue water fountains, nor crush blackberries with her hands so that she could go around telling people she had cut herself. She thought she would no longer be able to charge her friends to see her magnificent cuts and scrapes. Because Lilus had a habit of falling, and afterward sporting the inevitable bandage, she would walk alongside her friends and say:

"If you only knew how badly I fell . . . "

"Show me, Lilus, don't tease."

"I'll show you, but I charge."

"How much? I'll give you a kiss or a buck" (if it was a male).

"I prefer the buck."

Lilus would slowly pull back the adhesive tape and, after false cries of pain, would reveal little channels of red, black, and white.

And, remembering all the things she would no longer enjoy, Lilus wailed: "Mother, I don't want to go to the convent school!"

But Lilus went.

She left on a train, a very sad train of frequent heartrending hisses. A train so sad that it carries into the fog children who are lost like Lilus. A train of porters with smiles full of teeth, who eat God knows what. A train of pale women who play canasta and who think about the charity tea they will give when they arrive. A train of newly married couples, very cleanly bathed and embarrassed, thinking: "Should we sleep or . . . ?

A train for the sad and the happy, a train full of strange sounds . . . train of Lilus, the tormented girl on her way to the convent school.

Wheat fields! Fields of green and flowering trees!

A severe mansion surrounded by laughing things.

A house with the look of a happy widow!

Like those women you sometimes see on the street, stiff and dressed for mourning, but with cheeks like apples and dancing green eyes—that's how the nuns are. You imagine a much less horrible inside, beneath the gloomy black.

That's how the convent is, a cage full of little nuns who move like frightened birds, different from the rest of the world. They take steps that slide, quiet and sweet steps, lithe rabbit steps that barely skim the floor. In addition, the nuns always do the tiniest jobs, and assign a great deal of importance to the most insignificant things, as though on these things rests the order of the world: "The altar mantel is not smooth!" "Oh, Lord, it makes me twitch inside!" "We've go to straighten it quickly, before mass begins!"

Looking somewhat ghostly, Lilus's convent nuns are all skinny, with long legs, nervous gestures, and sweet, frightful moods. They are so tiny and skinny, they seem to have no gender. They are all called Sebastian, Louis, or Tarcisius. Nevertheless, something in them is courageous and endearing, a combination of decision and vacillation.

The first nun that Lilus saw was the Mother Gatekeeper. An agile dancer and singing mother, on whom Lilus mentally put gaudy pants.

The Mother Gatekeeper was intensely preoccupied with a beehive in the yard. She was constantly looking out at it, and always complained that the queen bee had stung her finger. Through a hole in the roof, rain would come into the Mother

Gatekeeper's room. It made her laugh: "Last night a frog came in. I made it a little bed alongside mine," she said. Her eyes reminded one of a statue's eyes, which never look on anything ugly. In a moving voice, she would sing the lamentations of Holy Week: "*Jerusalem, Jerusalem, convertete ad dominum deum nostrum Jesum.*" And her voice was like that of a child's, ringing out those sad and innocent melodies that make one think.

And Lilus loved her convent school.

There they taught her that in the world it is only the children who are close to truth and purity. They talked about heavenly bodies and planets, and the Milky Way. They told her that there are poisonous mushrooms, acrobats, and southerly and northerly winds. And angels with transparent wings that fly through space fulfilling harmonious orders. She learned about the Virgin, was filled with wonder, and crowned her with flowers.

They informed her that one day she would be an adult person, and that she could not be an old-clothes street peddler, because that was very badly thought of. Then they explained about "badly thought of" and being honorable. If she wanted to have children, she must certainly first seek a husband. And they told her about the professions. Being a millionaire is very convenient; being a gardener is not praiseworthy. They prepared her for her wedding night. She must bathe in rose water and put a spoonful of honey in her mouth. Then wait on the bedside for her husband, patient and submissive. And, above all, she must be dignified, very dignified. They taught her that she must love animals and not judge them, that she must not judge adultery, because it is what is most judged and least understood.

They told her a story from the Bible, about the slave Uzza and the ark that God had built of acacia wood, embossed in gold by the ablest artisans. The ark was transported on a cart by oxen from Carthinium to Jerusalem, and, at a moment when the cart was leaning dangerously too much toward one side of the road, Uzza grabbed the ark with his hand. And he fell dead because he touched the house of God. "David was irritated because Jehovah would punish in such a manner his faithful servant Uzza, and was afraid of God from that day forward."

Because of that story, Lilus understood that to be of God, she would have to give herself completely. She must understand Him and fear Him. And she believed in the signs. Perhaps in this life, that is the most important thing: Believe in the signs, as Lilus believed from that day forward.

The End

PART 2

OTHER STORIES

The Philosopher's Daughter

The sophists argue beneath the red light of intelligence. They join their heads over the metaphysical well, deepen their gaze as though pulling on fishing lines, and slowly begin to extract the problems. Once in a while one of them removes his eyeglasses and wipes them, in order to better contemplate the Master's expression. Others meditate, withdrawn into themselves, laboriously seeking the right moment to emit the most intelligent phrase of the evening. They barely breathe, while they drop extinguished cigarette butts from their yellowed fingertips. Even the curtains, heavy with static grandness, participate in the transcendent dialogue, the monotonous game of the intellectuals. The lamplight, subjected to the red screen, draws a lunar circle over the carpet and they are all careful to put their chairs within that circle, in order to feel embraced by the Master's sphere of intelligence.

"... Napoleon and surrealism, Chinese art and the Holy Trinity.... Should women be granted the right to voice participation in the amorous experience? Heaven forbid! The police, after all, are an abomination. Let us consult the books, let us go directly to the sources; culture, gentlemen, is a very serious matter. Which of you said a few moments ago, 'I only know I know nothing'" Silence. The Master has begun to speak again, that chief of this band of book-assaulters. With heavy voice, like one about to pronounce his last will and testament, he places the sharp point of his intelligence on each inert thought. And the accompanying subordinate, intelligent minds cease and relent, allowing themselves to swell little by little, their brains like sponges submerged in live waters. There is a moment when they can no longer lodge one more drop of talent, and their faces burst into smiles, except for one jealous young intellectual who does not give in to the Master's suggestion, and remains isolated and dry, on the fringes of the luminous circle, which he only touches with the toes of his feet. The Master's wisdom drowns his rancorous heart, while four miserable words move vaguely through the desert of his empty head.

In a shadowy corner that the voices and light do not reach, and seated on a small chair, is a pale young girl with matted hair, dreams and nightmares braided into her eyebrows—a girl who embroiders and often pricks her fingers with the needle. Lost in her solitude, she creates covers for her father's books from an irresponsibly orange cloth. She trims her covers—between the ridges of German metaphysics—with fine satin thread and her blue lack of calligraphy. From time to time she is summoned by her father, philosopher, chief, and Master. She rushes to clean out the ashtrays, collects remnants of stemware destroyed by a violent phrase, refills the glasses of port, and adds biscuits to a tray the indefatigable thinkers have left empty. She hears them speak but does not understand, when someone recites a poem she still does not understand, but when at least the words sound pretty she feels content.

And so life passes. Twice a week, while the afternoon sun

struggles with the thick curtains, or while rain falls softly, the writers gather for their extensive discussions. Outside, wind, rain, or rays of sunshine. Inside, big words, cigarette ashes, and salmon-colored book covers.

But one day the unforeseen occurs; fortune seems to smile on the jealous poet. Tired of fighting like a dwarf before the gigantic oratory of the Master, and feeling beaten down, he retreats. His four miserable words rest in the shadows, definitively opaqued by foreign brilliance. He resolves never to return to the gatherings, removes his chair from the circle of light, whereupon his eyes fall on a distant, dark corner. There sits the girl—in a new, sweet territory far from the dialectic walls, unprotected by ironic wire fences. The resentful one tunes his antennae toward that unprotected position of his luminous enemy. Taking advantage of an ardent discussion—a brusque exchange between the Master and his most qualified adversary—he furtively moves toward the girl and sits down at her side. The solitary daughter receives him with trembling. She stops smiling at her fairy godmother, at the enchanted carriage, at the crystal slipper and the well, and instead looks intently at her pricked fingertips. He begins to speak, to tell her that the pages of life are open for her, that they are more beautiful than those in fairy tales. He begins relating the tale of the inept rose and the enchanted songbird, whose melody slowly opened each of her petals. The philosopher's daughter feels afraid and leaves in search of more empty glasses and filled ashtrays.

Once again she fills the goblets with port and satiates the metaphysical hunger of the sophists with abundant filled biscuits. She dares to interrupt the reading of a poem by exclaiming in broken words, "Father, for heaven's sake, sirens are maidens!" She wishes to intervene in the discussion, stating that Confucius was an illiterate Chinese, that the battle of Austerlitz was only won because of a strategic error, and that poor Josephine grew bored waiting for Napoleon, who thought nothing of the present and only played his cards in terms of posterity, but she hears: "Child, be quiet!" And the unthinking and wise father returns his daughter to the now dangerous dark corner. He delivers her to the secular branch, like a ridiculous and unarmed Joan of Arc. *She* who only knew how to contemplate dead leaves and the cruelty of the wind that took them away; the elves that dance in the moonlight; and the witches for whom scholastic Latin is unknown. *She* was delivered into the hands of the cautious ruffian who would employ the embers of her delayed intelligence to light new, bewildering, and dazzling fires of sentimental artifice.

One day they go out for a stroll, while the philosopher writes an extensive refutation of a review penned by an evil man who attacked his most recent book. The jealous one planned a lengthy autumn walk, in an arboretum he had purposely chosen in order to disorient her. Trees blossomed from phrases, filled with accomplice leaves, with unhealthy flowers and forbidden fruit. The girl bit into apples that were no longer infantile. In languid awe she abandons her hand in his. A tenacious, proud bird had rendered her open and subjected. On the corners of unexpected streets, he invents incredible bakeries filled with meringues and cups of tea, as fragrant conclusions to autumn days. From his pockets he pulled more and more disturbing books. Pages that speak to the sleeping heart and want to fill it with vague platitudes. (Until then, the philosopher's daughter had only read fairy tales and the story of the voyage of the great historian and geographer José Pardiñas y Llanes through Persia, Mesopotamia, and other remote places.) To defend herself, she speaks of the mixed-blood slaves and of Queen Zenobia, and makes little boats with the paper napkins.

And the earth entered twilight. For the first time, the philosopher's daughter becomes aware of the sun's setting. She buys candleholders and mass leaflets and kneels in various places asking forgiveness with her lily in hand. Her indifference to those around her is exchanged for cordial solicitude. Friendly and generous, she seeks in extreme humility to purchase all evil that does not belong to her, all vileness shared without right. It serves only to conserve her personal freedom, to hide her culpable booty. Her expression shines on the outside, hiding the interior darkness.

Encircled by curtains, the conclave of wise ones continued, presided over by the indifferent philosopher, who was incapable of noticing, in the salmon covers that continued to protect his books, the reflection of that eloquent flush from time to time over the girl's face. Twice a week, the sophists lit the red light of intelligence and became shipwrecked in the thick sea of readings, declaring in a chorus of inebriated voices: "Me and the other; being and time; experience of death; *Parerga un Paralipomena*; let us prolegomenon a theory of mutual incomprehension; Hölderlin and the verbal impossibility; Ezra Pound and the confusion of sources; Neruda and chaotic enumeration . . . "

And the traitor poet kept attending the gatherings. He sat at the Master's table like a Judas. The philosopher's daughter received the perpetrator at the door but did not give him away. The jealous one entered the parlor of the intellectuals like a mad rush of horses. His armor and cleavers first destroyed the girl's heart, then continued their devastation throughout the house. Each furnishing the poet touched fell to the floor in pieces. The girl had to reconstruct them piece by piece quickly, before his imagination could destroy the final details. His cup of coffee evaporated in his hand and she had to take great care to bring him back to reality and prevent the others from becoming aware of his many destructions. However, all remained unknowing.

Happy, victorious, inevitably, he now took part in the conversations, and his four unspoken words came out suddenly, brutally halting all aggressive discussion. They looked at him benevolently, then in a stupor. The Master approached him timidly, and gave him a pat on the shoulder. And he was pronounced a knight. The savage rush of horses then became more powerful than ever, and the girl felt that her error was justified by the general approbation of him. Trumpets sounded among the clinching of golden spurs, and the poet appeared in newly acquired, magnificent armor, brandishing a sword of infallible edge. His resplendent spurs ingrained themselves forever in his infantile and badly attained conscience.

But when they were alone, she was happy. She gave in to her love, supposing that in this life the only thing that really counts is the gratuitous and scary concession of oneself. Reproaches were quickly extinguished in the flower of her lips because he knew how to terminate them. His power was unbreakable and alien to real life, he triumphed over all things, and she was no more than a stream in which he washed his guilty hands.

One day the unforeseen again occurred. In his incommensurable ambition, the jealous one invented a fifth word. A word of possession and dominion, which hurt the Master for the first time, not in his vanity or self-love, but in his very flesh. The philosopher looked outside of himself for the first time, and discovered the eyes of his daughter filled with tears. There was no manner of reducing her to the verbal space of a brilliant phrase; she was there, unaccountable, mute and hurting. This was life. And life was about to depart forever from his side, taken by that intrusive hand, in which he himself had placed a violent weapon. Outside, the light of this last real day would not extinguish. Inside, encircled by curtains, the universe of grand words, cigarette ashes, and salmon-covered books became smaller.

The philosopher's daughter said goodbye to her friend and carefully shut the door. But the final sound of his carriage became anchored to her heart. As she averted her gaze, she saw the pieces of a furnishing and, now without terror, she rectified it. The philosopher asked, in humility, for more port and biscuits. The young minds moved together again into the circle of red light and, more for the sake of custom than by conviction, harmonized a hymn to culture and learning.

Fifth Call

At first she did not even see the room. She felt nothing more than Rodrigo and his manly, forceful kisses. They knew that no action by the other could be disconcerting; they had pushed beyond the limits of their own bodies. Together they breathed the same air, the air compressed into their embrace. And words of love—that awkward, stuttering language—surged.

"..."

"..."

"Are you cold?"

"No."

And Rodrigo picked up the sheets and the frayed blanket. He pulled these around her as though she were a child, even his daughter.

"Rodrigo, you are my father and my mother and my brother and my sister and my children and my earth. Rodrigo... Rodrigo, you are the cathedral and the plaza, Rodrigo, you are Las Delicias Restaurant and table seven and the plastic flowers and the blonde who waits on us."

They felt immensely grateful and this made them return one to the other, to bury themselves in an embrace because nothing better could ever be provided them. She felt so intensely happy that her eyes suddenly filled with tears. Rodrigo did not ask her anything. He knew why she cried.

Outside it was raining. She thought that as they left huge drops of water would fall on her face and hair; she felt pleased— they would walk holding hands, laughing, smiling, constantly seeking each other's eyes.

Someone walked along the corridor.

"Who is coming?"

"Don't be so frightened," he smiled. "I have the key right here."

"But the door is so flimsy."

"Don't be a scaredy cat."

They heard knocking.

"See, I told you."

"It's not here, it's next door."

"But, why?"

"They must have taken too long."

The noise at the door was offensive and terrible.

"What a rude way of knocking!"

"They're not going to open, don't worry."

The hotel manager would surely knock the door in. Julia thought of the lovers still locked in embrace. And all because they had taken too long! They, on the other hand, never delayed. Rodrigo sat on the bed and stroked her hair.

"Do we have to go already, Rodrigo?"

"Yes, you know we do. I have an appointment."

As she dressed, Julia looked at the room. One wall was pink, the other cream colored, the roof brownish-cream, and the bathroom with no door a strident green. The bed with its dirty comforter barely fit in this small room. The only other furnishing was a tarnished spit pot.

They laughed as they looked at each other in the mirror.

"Don't we make a great couple?"

They dressed each other, brushed each other's hair, passing the comb back and forth. Julia kissed him and then got onto the bed and under the covers all dressed. Rodrigo reached for her and they again tremblingly found each other.

"Julia."

"Yes, I know, it's late. Very late."

"And it could take time to find where I left the car."

Always as they left, Rodrigo would drive quickly, nervously, cursing at the stalled traffic, with his face hard, fixed on red lights, as though the power of his look through the windshield could push the stopped cars. Sometimes he held her hand, the only recognition of her presence in the midst of multitudes. Julia was always surprised to notice his profile. He looked older then—he had the face of a man of action—a face Julia did not recognize.

"What are you thinking about, Julia?"

"The return."

"You always anticipate things."

"It's because we are leaving."

Rodrigo put an arm around her shoulders and kissed her on the forehead.

"Oh no, it's the goodbye kiss."

And she covered her face with the pillow.

"Julia!"

"Rodrigo, I no longer do anything to save myself."

This was a language that was way over Rodrigo's head.

"Rodrigo, cover my heart with this blanket."

He gazed at her without understanding. He walked around the bed, buttoning a last button on his shirt, and smiled trying to figure her out.

"Rodrigo, I wish you were a kangaroo and you could carry me with you always in your pouch."

Julia waited for him to say something, something that would fill the emptiness. Rodrigo was necessary to her for existing, for getting up quickly in the mornings, so that dirt did not smell like a dead child, and so that nothing seemed irreparable. "Get undressed, my love, for we are going to die!"

As Rodrigo said goodbye at the doorway of her house, he would always say: "I'll give you a holler just as soon as I can."

Julia assented with a pitiful smile, nodding her head. Her expression no longer contained her, not the Julia of the multicolored room, nor she of the thin door being beaten by an irascible fist.

"I'll call you . . . tomorrow . . . at . . . "

"Yes, yes," Julia approved.

Meanwhile, there was a lot to remember. Like when they took walks with their eyes raised toward the familiar buildings with porous facades where sunshine and balconies nested, vines escaping from pots incarcerating seeds and hung like cages, birds picking at the spots of afternoon rays, the watering pots, the smells of honeysuckle and spearmint. Below, the streets joined together, Jesús María, Regina, Mesones, Justo Sierra, Santa Efigenia, San Idelfonso, la Santísima, Topacio, Loreto, and the last two, Belisario Domínguez and Leandro Valle y Cuba, which dead-ended at the lovely plaza of Santo Domingo.

"Oh, Rodrigo, a room in this neighborhood for us! Can you imagine what it would be like to open the window onto this view?"

They stopped below the sign, "For rent, information at Academia #19." The small room, on Moneda Street, faced a brick wall—a hot and red fortress, stubborn with hope.

They almost always found benevolent doormen: "Actually they are offices. Since these were old houses, the bathroom is upstairs."

"It doesn't matter, it doesn't matter."

"The rent is three hundred and fifty pesos."

"So much? But why?"

"Prices have really gone up around here." They always looked at them with sympathy. "Of course if you speak to the owner, maybe he can bring it down a little."

One day as they strolled, Rodrigo tripped and knocked over an entire box of soda bottles in front of a shop, although almost all of them were empty.

"Let me pay you for this," he said to the shop owner.

But the fat man did not charge him. To the contrary, he invited them to come by again the next day, she with her windswept hair, a purse strap on her shoulder and a wadded-up sweater, all disheveled, and he who knew how to speak to everyone with that buddy style, casual and dreamy.

"You know, Rodrigo, I think they would like to have us as neighbors."

They walked hand in hand, without separating even when people pushed together on the sidewalk. If they absolutely had to let go, their fingers then sought each other, guiding ship-wrecked, anxious hands. On Cinco de Mayo Street there was a massive building sustained by two huge arches. Julia loved it above all other buildings. Inside, it contained offices and more offices: tailor shops and notaries and loan shops and rental offices. To the side, the door opening like a huge golden mouth, was a Chinese restaurant; round, greasy pancakes were piled up in their paper molds in the window below a bright heat lamp. In all of the cafes there were baked goods, rolls, candies, items that fit in the palm of the hand. Announcements for beer and daily specials were scrawled with white chalk on blackboards, often with misspelled words: *peas* with no *a* and *frijoles* written with a *g* instead of a *j*, and *flan* written with an accent mark that should not be there.

Rodrigo and Julia took it all in, then they followed some narrow, wooden stairs to the top.

"You want it for an office?"

Rodrigo muttered who-knows-what; Julia would have answered: "No sir, it's just that we have nowhere to go."

She thought of a lamp with an ancient shade, one of those with a fringe, that hangs from the ceiling, and of a window that opens to the street so she can see the lamp from outside and would know, when she sees it lit, that Rodrigo is there waiting for her. "Oh, Rodrigo, from here you can hear the cathedral bells!"

"We've got to get organized and get ourselves a place."

But they both knew they would not, because they did not desire it enough. Because for Rodrigo it was sufficient to say to Julia, "I'll give you a holler!" And Julia always agreed to whatever, although maybe some night it would be she who would holler, even yell, a yell like a vanquished animal, or of a dog being kicked, one who runs away with the tail between its legs. No, not a dog, a bitch, bitch of herself without even a puppy to lick or who would lick her wounds. A yell that would break everything into pieces, even this: this that they thought was their love, their meager love that jiggled here and there, shaking in their hands along the streets, and that one day they would carry on their backs like an unbearable load that perhaps they would share only because they did not want to set it down, or say *you* carry it for a while.

"What are you thinking about, Julia?"

It had grown dark.

Julia did not answer. She said in a low, very low voice almost to herself: "Get undressed, my love, for we are going to die."

"Julia, come on now, let's go."

Outside, as they left, Julia looked back and noticed the neon sign that read: "Hotel Solitude."

Happiness

Yes, my darling, yes, I am here beside you, my love. Yes, I love you, of course, my darling, yes, I know, you tell me not to tell you so often. I know, I know, they are big words, for a one-time occasion and for all of life. On the other hand, you never call me darling, sweetheart, my love, my dearest; you don't believe in heaven, my darling. My love, take care of me, may I never leave these four walls that enclose me, forget me here in your arms, wrap me up with your eyes, cover me with your eyes, save me, protect me, darling, my happiness, don't go. Look, there is that word again, I trip over it at each step. Give me your hand, for later you will say, happiness, you were here with us; yes, you will say it, but I want to think it right now, say it right now.

Look, the sun comes in, the heat and those fierce branches of ivy with their small, strong leaves that cling to the heat of the window and continue growing in your room and entangle themselves with us. I need them, I want them, they are our bindings, because I, my love, need you, you are necessary. That is it, you are necessary and you know it, you necessary man who never says my name. I have no name at your side and when you say this and that, my name never appears and you reject my words, like happiness. My darling, I love you, because you are wise and you don't like to name anything, although happiness is there, lying in wait, with its happy name, which remains suspended in air, above us, in the shifting afternoon light, and if I don't name it, it dissipates and later shadows appear, and I say to you, my darling, give me back the light.

Then with the points of your fingers you go over my body from my face to my toes, along a path you choose, knowing me, and I remain motionless, on one side, with my back to you as your fingertips trace my flanks, from the tips of my toes to my front side; you stop momentarily at the hips and you say, you have lost weight, and I think of a skinny horse, belonging to the comedian Cantinflas, who hangs his feathered hat on its rump, because I, my love, am your nag, and can no longer gallop and await you vigilantly. Yes, I watch you while I say, don't go, you have nothing to do but be here with me, with your hand on my hips. No, we're not leaving, tie me up, put your shirt on me; you laugh because it looks so large on me, don't laugh, go get some ice water from the kitchen because it is hot and we are thirsty, come on, go. No, wait, I'll go; no, I'm going; okay, go on, wait, don't get up, it's my turn, now I have gone running for the water and here I am again at your side, you on the bed, naked and free as the sunset. Here, drink some too, drink the illuminating light, can't you see, I don't want the sun to leave while we drink happiness, I don't want the sun to leave nor for you to stop stretching that way, outside of time, as night begins to come in through the window, our window. Look, cover it with your hand, don't let the night come in, may there never cease to be a window, although you can cover the sun for me with one finger. Yes, my love, yes, I am here, your window to the world, cover me with your hand, close me off like the sun. You can make night, you breathe and air no longer comes through the window, how happy we are, look how cold you are, the window is immo-bilized like me, static forever, cover me with your hand—oh, what forgetfulness of everything! The window maintains our only exit, our communication with heaven.

I love you, my darling, let's go to heaven while the neighbor lady goes out to hose down the patio, her patio, a patio for washing, while here in your patio no one washes and there are wild weeds in the washing place, they are tall and the wind makes them sway because there are no clothes to make sway on the clotheslines above. Remember when in October a dandelion appeared, a small one, barely there, and I felt it sway above my belly, between my tangled hair—tangled, messy and sad and yellow like a small abandoned garden. A garden on the outskirts of town that encircles us and comes in through the window to this small abode, this bread-box of a house, where I rest in its bosom of tenderness. A house of gold, round like hope, *Cinderella, dressed in yellow, went downstairs to meet a fella.* House of hap-piness, have mercy on us, keep us within your strong walls, don't open the door, don't leave us unsheltered, we have filled you with words, look, look, I just provided another. My love, my darling, my sweetheart, my life, the humidity increases and I no longer know how to quiet your heartbeats. I am still, see, I am not like a grasshopper, don't say I am like a flea with clothes on, I am not moving, see. Why do you always say, "Be still," but I am not doing anything, I just ask you if you want to sleep, and you pull me to you, I embrace you and cradle myself within your arms, and I know that you don't want to sleep, you simply want us to be still, quiet and meek while the earth's heat rises, and grows, pulsating. I love you, my darling, we are a couple, the perfect archetype, I rest my head on your chest like a medallion, I inscribe myself in you. Word of honor, word of love, stamped on your mouth, there are flames of fire on your lips, flames that suddenly located my substance. Now we celebrate the Pentecost, the union of word and substance, but we are never going to die, right? because no one loves as we love each other, no one loves this way because you and me, we are us and no one can come against us here enclosed within your chest and my body. Let me see you, you are inside me, look at me through my eyes, don't let them close, don't sleep, my love, don't let sleep take you. Your eyelids are drooping, look at me, let me look at you, don't leave me, may the sun also not leave, may it not weaken, may it not dip into the horizon, don't give in like the light, the sun, leave everything as it was on my virgin skin. Look, you can see me better now than before because the sun is setting, because you are setting also, and I am here telling you, don't go, last forever, last like the sun I saw as a girl with eyes wide open, burning me, prolonging until I saw darkness, dark as the conclusion of those fairy tales that end in the happy-ever-after routines of princes who are very happy and have many, many children.

Don't fall asleep, don't fall asleep, I say, anxiously, invariably, without a "later." Because there is no later for us if you leave me. But you won't leave me ever, you have to return to pick me up, to unite the pieces again on this bed where I am substance; you can't leave me because a part of me would be missing from you forever, like a piece of a puzzle that is missing and destroys the picture as a whole—the whole of me, the life you have given me and that you cannot remove because you would die, you would be blind and unable to find me—me, limping, missing a limb from you, without words, mute, with the word "end" sealing my lips, the end of all stories, there is no longer any story, I won't tell the tale anymore, nothing else matters. Things transform, there is no longer any "more" upon the earth.

Look, the mosquito net on the window is punctured. I look at our mementos, the two butterflies on the wall with their china-paper wings—in yellow, pink, orange—the spinning top and the painted wooden bird you bought on the street that Friday when everything began, the Friday that was yellow and strident pink like this little bird that pecks at us since then, a child's toy like the paper butterflies that fly in the park before the real ones come out of their cocoons, like those you crucified in our previous rented room—big ones, with marvelous, transparent blue wings. You put pins through them, one on top of another, a stick pin that hurt me and I asked you how you could do it. Just by doing it, you said, and you pierced happiness, you petrified it there on the wall, happy. Again that word, I repeat it, come back, come back and I'll repeat it. You get irritated and say, once again the needle in the haystack to the greedy straws of happiness, don't you understand? No, I don't understand, help me out of this discord, help me walk through those fields of God's wheat with the pin stuck through me, now without the other butterfly. Don't you know that no one belongs to anyone (you say), that what we have is enough, enough and even miraculous? Yes, yes, yes, my love, it is a miracle, don't close your eyes, I understand now, don't close yourself away, don't sleep, come out and look at me. You are tired and in a little while you are going to sleep, you are going to the river, and I will remain on the shore, the shore that we walked together. Remember, under the eucalyptus trees, us strolling to accompany the movement of the river, under the leaves, under the rays of light? I am open to all wounds, I opened my virgin self to you, I open my mouth and give myself to you, even my teeth strong like tools. I am no longer ashamed of myself. Okay, I lied, I am a little ashamed and I tell all the nuns I encounter that I like thorns as well as roses. Below their birdlike bodies with long black skirts, where they play with their rosaries, the wind and the light cannot vibrate between their legs. Get out of here, birds of bad omen, get out of here, weeds of life, gloomy cobwebs in the corners, full of dust. Leave me, you narrow-minded views, spying through cracks, doors about to shut, all of you go to mourning. You are like brooms, let me sweep the world with you—you who swept so many little colored papers from my soul.

But you, my love, remain here with me. I wish I had known you older, sitting at the fireside knitting my need to await your return—although you would never have arrived—and humming to myself the same old song, *when I was young, he would remain sleeping at the foot of my window.* Although it is not true, because today you came early, before I had time to get up, and you put your hand on the door handle, and turned the lock, and I liked your pants with the deformed pockets, pockets that seem to carry all the accidents of life, and your own thoughts, like wrappings of caramel converted to little balls. Your thoughts, darling, tell me what you think, my love, tell me what you are thinking right now, but right now when you seem to be by yourself alone, forgetting that I am here with you. My love, what are you thinking? I always ask the same thing, do you love me? You have fallen asleep, I know you are going to sleep and I am going to get dressed without making noise, and I'll close the door carefully as I leave, in order to keep you there wrapped in the tepid red and ochre of the afternoon light, because you have fallen asleep and you no longer belong to me and you did not take me with you, you left me behind, this afternoon when the sun and the heat came in through the window. And I am going to walk and walk and walk, and the neighbor lady will see me from her door, observe me with her disapproving look because only once in a while do I venture along this path. I will walk as far as the eucalyptus, until I am completely exhausted, until I accept that you are a body there asleep and I another here walking, and that the two of us are irremediably, irremediably, totally, and desperately alone.

You Arrive by Nightfall

"But, don't you suffer?"

"Me?"

"Yes, you."

"Sometimes, a little, when my shoes are too tight. . . . "

"I am referring to your situation, madam" (putting stress on the word *madam*, he let it sink into the depths of hell, *m-a-d-a-m*) "and the suffering you cause. Doesn't it also make you suffer?"

"No."

"Was it much effort for you to reach this place in time? Did your family go to a lot of effort for you?"

The woman squirmed in her chair and her green eyes stopped interrogating the public ministry official. She looked down at the floor and examined the pointed toes of her shoes; they were not too tight, they were daily-wear shoes.

"Don't you work for a center that owes its existence to the principles of the Mexican Revolution? Haven't you benefited from the same? Don't you enjoy the privileges of a social class that only yesterday arrived from the province and today receives schooling, medical attention, social welfare? You have been able to succeed thanks to your work. Oh, I have forgotten that your concept of work is a little curious!"

The woman's protests came in a clear voice, although her intonation was infantile. "I have my nursing credential. I can show you my diploma, right now in fact, if we go to my house."

"Your house?" the official replied sarcastically, "your house? Which, of all of them?"

The courtroom consisted of old, deteriorated wood, painted and repainted, while the official's face strangely did not look so old, despite his drooped shoulders and his constant shrugs, which accentuated them. His voice was old, his intentions old, he had clumsy gestures and a habit of fixating his eyes on her through his glasses as though he were a schoolteacher irritated with his pupil for a badly prepared lesson. "Things," she thought, "contaminate people; this man is like a piece of paper, a drawer, an inkpot. Poor thing." She glanced back at the rows of seats behind her; no one else was in the room. Except for a police officer near the exit door who was scratching his balls. That door opened and a short woman walked in, reached up to the judge's desk, and handed him a file. As he scanned the document, he scolded her in a fierce tone: "The crimes have to be specifically spelled out. And at the end, you always forget to type the statement, 'Effective Suffrage, No Re-Election.' Do not let this happen again. Please!"

Once they were alone again, the detained woman asked in a high voice, "Could I call home?"

The judge was about to repeat in his sarcastic tone, "Which home?" but instead he preferred to emit a negative sound by rounding his mouth in such a manner that all the wrinkles converged into the shape of a chicken butt.

"No."

"Why?"

"Because-we-are-in-the-midst-of-sentencing. You are being charged with a crime."

"So if I need to go to the bathroom, do I have to hold it?"

"My God, is this woman mentally retarded, or what? But if she is, how could she have completed her studies and received her diploma?" the official mused, then asked with renewed curiosity:

"Who do you want to call?"

"My father."

"Your father, *my-fa-ther*," he mocked. "So on top of everything else you have a father."

"Yes," she said, swinging her legs, "yes, my daddy is alive and well."

"Really? And does your father know what kind of daughter he has?"

"I look like him," said the woman-girl with a smile. "We have always looked alike, always, always."

"Really? And when, pray tell, do you have time to see him?"

"On the weekends; I try to spend the weekends with him." Her sweet tone caused the police officer to stop scratching. "Every weekend?"

"Well, not all of them. Once in a while there is an emergency and I cannot go. But I always telephone him to let him know."

"And the others, do you advise them by telephone?"

"Certainly."

"Please stop swinging your legs and control yourself, madam, we are in a court of law."

She stared with candid eyes at the empty rows of seats behind her, the plywood counter painted gray, and the extremely tall filing cabinets stamped "government property." Earlier, as she was led through the offices outside the courtroom, she felt the laminate desks practically overpower her with their stacks of files piled in disorder, some with a white card marking something in their midst. In fact, she almost knocked over one of the taller piles dangerously stacked on the corner of a desk at which a chubby woman—snuggled up to the desk—ate her lunch. Apparently, she had just taken a few bites out of the sandwich in her hands and was now furtively adding large, messy strips of avocado to it, which had been sliced with her letter-opener. She also noticed the chipped tile floor—gray and sordid-looking despite daily mopping—and the windows, which looked out to the street, extremely small windows with thick bars in close proximity. The glass in these windows, which had apparently never been washed, reflected a sad, grayish light. It was obvious no one cared about this edifice; everyone likely fled as soon as they finished their work. No air entered these offices except for that emitted as the front door opened and then immediately closed. The chubby woman returned her half-eaten sandwich to a paper bag and placed it in a drawer that also contained a banana, all apparently stored to be consumed later; the drawer shut with a snapping sound. Then, without washing her hands, she turned to face the typewriter.

All of the typewriters were tall, very old, and with ribbons that could not rewind on their own. The chubby woman now introduced her finger, or at least a fingernail, into the carriage and started rewinding the ribbon. When she tired of doing this, she pulled her ink-stained finger out, took a fountain pen out of the middle drawer of the desk, and inserted it into the center of the ribbon carriage. The task completed, and now with her glasses on, she proceeded to initiate her work, not caring that the detained person in this anteroom might hear her reading the official record. "The witness affirms that he was not in the home at the time of the incident. . . . " The woman paused to adjust the carbon pages, moistening her thumb and index finger. All documents were apparently prepared with ten carbon copies but only five retained because there were numerous sheets of crumpled, used carbon paper with the initials for "Federal District" in the square, gray garbage can. "Gosh!" she thought to herself, "what a lot of carbon paper; why would they want so many copies?" Everyone in the court offices area seemed immune to criticism or even self-criticism; some scratched their sides, others their armpits, a woman adjusted a bra strap, grimacing. The workers also grimaced as they sat down, but then they got up again and moved to another desk to consult some piece of information that made them scratch their noses or pass their tongue repeatedly over their teeth, seeking some prodigious milligram of an object that, when discovered, might then be removed with the little finger. Essentially, no one in the offices seemed to notice their own actions, much less those of others.

"Tell them to send García to take down the declaration," the officiating judge suddenly barked.

"How many copies will they make?" the accused asked.

Nothing seemed to perturb the clean look on her face; there were no shadows, no hidden intention behind the sparkling surface of her gaze. The official had to reply:

"Ten."

"I knew it!" she exclaimed triumphantly.

"Well, how many times have you been detained?"

"Never before, this is my first experience. I know because I noticed while I waited in the anteroom. I am very observant," she added with a satisfied laugh.

"You must be, to be able to sustain such a situation for seven years."

The woman smiled, a fresh, innocent smile, and the judge thought: "No wonder." He was about to smile himself, but instead, he thought: "I need to keep this as serious and impersonal as possible, but how can I when this woman seems to be playing, she crosses and uncrosses her legs, revealing golden, round, beautifully shaped knees?"

"Let's see, your name?"

"Esmeralda Loyden."

"Age?"

"Twenty-seven."

"Place of birth?"

"Mexico City."

"A City girl, huh?"

"Yes," Esmeralda smiled again.

"Address?"

"Mirto Street, number 27, apartment 3."

"Neighborhood?"

"Santa María la Rivera."

"Postal code?"

"Four."

"Profession?"

"Nurse. Oh, your honor, the address I have just given you is my father's address." She shook her head of profuse curly locks. "You have the other addresses."

"Okay, now we are going to look at the charges. Are you getting this down, García?"

"Yes, sir."

"Catholic?"

"Yes."

"Practicing?"

"Yes."

"How often?"

"I always go to mass on Sundays, sir."

"Really? And how do you feel about that?"

"Well, sir, I especially enjoy the singing masses."

"And sunrise masses? You should like those best!" the old official roared hoarsely.

"Those are only once a year, but I also enjoy them."

"Really? And who do you attend mass with?"

"With my father. I always spend Christmas with him."

Esmeralda's eyes widened, green as new, untouched grass. "God, she even seems like a virgin," he thought.

"Let's see, García. Ready for pronouncement of sentencing in case number 132-6763, dictated at the 32nd Precinct Tribunal, for the crime of five counts of bigamy."

"Five, sir?"

"That's right, five, isn't it?"

"Yes, Your Honor, but only one is accusing her."

"But she's married to all five, right?"

"Yes, sir."

"Get this in writing, then—let's see, the first declaration is from the city of Querétaro, state of Querétaro. It reads: 'United Mexican States. In the name of the Republic of Mexico, and as State Judge for Civil Matters, I hereby make known to those bearing witness of this document that in the Official Record under "Marriages" in my jurisdiction, on page 18 of the year 1948, government permit number 8577, file 351.2-49-82756, and the date of June 12th, 1948, at 8 p.m., the citizen Pedro Lugo Alegría and Miss Esmeralda Loyden appeared before me in the act of officiating matrimony by rule of Conjugal Society.' Did you get all of that, García? There are four acts like this one, all duly legalized and sealed. The only difference in each is the name of the male citizen taking oath, because the female subject—disgustingly—always remains the same: Esmeralda Loyden. Here is a document signed and legalized in Cuernavaca, Morelos; another in Chilpancingo, Guerrero; another in Los Mochis, Sinaloa; and the fifth in Guadalajara, Jalisco. As we can see, besides being bigamous, madam, you do like to travel."

"Not even that much, sir, they're the ones who . . . well, because of the nature of the honeymoon."

"Of course."

"Yes, your honor, for my part, I would just as soon have remained in Mexico City," she added in her melodious voice.

Once again the chubby woman with the file entered the room. The judge, exasperated, grabbed the file in a brusque manner and read aloud from the typed document: "'. . . based on visual inspections and professional observation, the damages caused during the course of actions committed as stated in the previous document . . . ,' and from there on continue yourself, as long as it is not more than one page. And here we go again! Once again you forgot to put in the statement at the end, 'Effective Suffrage, No Re-Election,' as I have told you countless times. Now, don't get so distracted. Don't let this happen again. Please."

It was obvious the judge was finally ready to return to Esmeralda Loyden's case because as soon as the dwarf shut the door, he hurriedly stated:

"The names of the male parties, García, should appear on the juridical order in strict alphabetical order: Carlos González Ramos, Pedro Lugo Alegría, Gabriel Mercado Zepeda, Livio Martínez Cruz, Julio Vallarta Blanco." One, two, three, four, five—the judge counted to himself. "Therefore, you would be Mrs. Esmeralda Loyden de González, Esmeralda Loyden de Lugo, Esmeralda Loyden de Martínez, Esmeralda Loyden de Mercado, Esmeralda Loyden de Vallarta . . . Um-hmm. How does that sound to you, García?"

"Okay."

"What do you mean, 'okay'?"

"The names are correct, Your Honor, but the only one who filed an accusation is Pedro Lugo Alegría."

"I am not asking you that, García, I am making a point based on the moral, legal, social, and political implications of this case, which seems to have escaped your sensibilities."

"Oh, okay, Your Honor!"

"Have you ever, García, come across a similar case in all of your life?"

"No, Your Honor, well, not in respect to a woman anyway, because men . . . " and García let out a long, shrill whistle.

"Let's see what the accused has to say. But first, madam Esmeralda, please permit me a strictly personal question: Didn't you ever confuse Julio with Livio?"

Esmeralda, with a fixed gaze, seemed a small creature before a kaleidoscope of deep, flowing waters as transparent as her eyes. Apparently, it was a kaleidoscope only she could see. Irritated, the judge repeated his question.

"Do I confuse them? Oh, but, Your Honor, they are each so different!"

"Didn't you ever have a doubt, or stumble?"

"How could I have?" she responded energetically. "I respect them too much."

"Not even in the dark?"

"I don't understand, sir."

Esmeralda fixed her tranquil, transparent gaze on the older man for so long he was forced to cease his authoritative stare. "This is incredible," he thought, "now I am the one who is going to have to beg forgiveness of her." He barked: "Did you submit to the gynecological exam with the court doctor?"

"But, why?" García protested. "This is not a case of rape."

"Oh, that's right, they're the ones who should be required to have an exam," the judge laughed, gesticulating in a vulgar manner.

The woman smiled also, as though he were not talking about her; she smiled politely, to accompany the old man, and this disconcerted him even more.

"So it was five?" He tapped his fingers on the filthy wooden table.

"All five needed me."

"And you were prodigiously available."

"They felt a very considerable urgency."

"And children? Did you have children?" he asked, almost politely.

"How could I have children? They're my children, I care for them and take care of them in every way, I would not have time for others."

The judge could not proceed; the jokes of double entendre, the insults, the ingenious comments all went over her head. And García was a beast, a total waste; he even seemed to feel solidarity for the accused. The judge would have to wait for happy hour in order to tell his buddies stories about this woman's life and that forever-sweet, smiling expression permanently on her face.

"I suppose you met the first one in the park."

"How did you know? Yes, I met Carlos in the Sunken Garden Park; I was reading that novel of José Emilio Pacheco's, *You will die far from home*."

"So you like to read?"

"No, that's the only novel I have ever read, and it was only because I met the author." Esmeralda's voice took on an enthusiastic tone. "I thought he was a priest, you see, we were on the same bus and as we got off at the same stop, I asked him, 'Father, give me your blessing.' He became nervous, he even began sweating, and he extended his arm and gave me a black book, saying: 'Here, so that you can see that I am not a priest, here is a copy of my book.'"

"Okay, and what happened with Carlos?"

"Pedro, excuse me, Carlos, sat on the bench where I was reading and asked me if it was a good book, and that is how everything began. Ah, no! It was because he had something in his eye—you know how February is the month for dust storms—and I offered to take it out because he was tearing up. Since I am a nurse, well, I told him, I can do that for you. And I got it out. And by the way, sir, I have been noticing for some time that your left eye is watery. Why don't you tell your wife to put in some eye drops from distilled chamomile, but not the dried kind, use fresh chamomile. Tell your wife to tell them to give her several flowering ones, and the pot she boils it in should be totally clean. Then all you have to do is tilt your head back and keep it that way about ten minutes so that it penetrates well. You'll see how well it heals your eye, that is, if you use the pure flower of the chamomile."

"So you're the type that offers herself . . . in assistance."

"Yes, Your Honor, that is my natural reaction. Also with Gabriel the same thing happened; he had burned his arm; he had it in quite bad shape with one boil after another, and I cured it, it was my job to bandage it, orders from Dr. Carrillo. Once he got well, he told me I don't know how many times that what he most wanted in life, besides me, was his right arm because . . . "

Esmeralda Loyden's five accounts were similar; one followed another, with very few variations. She described her marriages with glossy and confident eyes; sometimes she was completely and innocently fatuous in her assertions: "Without me, Pedro cannot live. He doesn't even know where his shirts are." The officiating judge felt the words *perversion*, *perfidy*, and *depravity*, and *supreme shame* trembling on his lips, but he never had the opportunity to emit them; they remained burning on his tongue. With Esmeralda they lost all meaning. Her account was simple and direct: Mondays belonged to Pedro, Tuesdays to Carlos, and so on until she completed the week, English-style of course, because on Saturdays and Sundays she had to wash and iron her and their clothes and prepare a stew for Pedro, the one with the pickiest requests. When an emergency came up, a birthday, a holiday, a day in the country, then she had to give up her working weekend. Oh, but they all accepted, as long as they could see her, and she always gave as her one condition that she not have to abandon her career as a nurse.

"And are they fine with your granting them only one day each?"

"Sometimes they get a little more. Anyway, they also work. Carlos is a traveling salesman, but he always makes certain he is home onTuesdays without fail; Gabriel sells insurance, he also travels, and is so intelligent they have offered him work at IBM."

"Hasn't one of them desired a child?"

"They have never voiced it strongly. When they have brought it up, I respond that we only have been married a few years, that our love needs to mature."

"And they accept?"

"Yes, it would seem so."

"Well, it would seem that this little theatrical act has ended because they have accused you, madam."

"That was Pedro—he has always been moody, and too easily excited, but down deep, Your Honor, he's a good guy, he has such a good heart, you'll see, he got a little carried away but he will settle down. You'll see."

"I won't see anything because you are confined to jail; for eight days you have been locked up alone. Aren't you aware, madam Esmeralda, didn't it bother you to be so confined?"

"Not so much, everyone here has been so kind; and besides, one loses track of time. I have slept at least eight hours each night, because I was really very tired."

"I can imagine. Then, it would seem, things never seem bad to you?"

"Nope. I have never gone to sleep with anything bad in my mind."

And, the truth was, the young woman looked very good, with healthy skin, clean and fresh, her eyes brimming with radiance; she even had a calm demeanor. Oh, and her hair! It had a special sheen to it, hair as fine as that of a newborn animal, so fine it made one want to caress it as well as pull her snotty little nose. The judge felt he was about to explode; he had had enough. He raised his voice:

"And, don't you realize that you lived in the most absolute promiscuity; that you deceived, that-you-de-ceive; that you are not only immoral but also amoral; that you have no principles; that you are pornographic; that yours is a mental illness; that your ingenuity is a—a sign of—of imbe-cili-ty?" He was beginning to stutter. "People like you destroy our society at its very roots, you destroy the nuclear family, you are a social menace! Don't you see all of the wrong you have caused with your irresponsible conduct?"

"Wrong to whom?" Esmeralda whined.

"To the men you deceive, to yourself, to society, to the principles of the Mexican Revolution!"

"Why? The days we shared are all happy, harmonious, they hurt no one."

"And the deceit?"

"What deceit? One thing is not to tell and another is to deceive."

"You are crazy. The court psychiatrist will surely prove that."

"Really? But what is going to happen to me?"

"Ah, so you're finally thinking about that? This is the first time you have actually thought about what is going to happen to you."

"That's true, Your Honor, it has never been my way to worry about things."

"I don't know what kind of woman you are, I do not understand you. either you're mentally weak, or, or, I don't know, a fallen woman."

"A fallen woman?" Esmeralda became very serious. "Tell that to Pedro."

"To Pedro, to Juan, and to many others, to any of your five husbands, who once they know it are going to think the same."

"I don't believe they will think the same, they are each so different; I don't even think the same as you nor could I."

"My God, aren't you aware of your terrible state of conscience?" The judge slammed his fist down on the table, making dust fly everywhere. "You are a wh—. You behave like a prost—" (curiously, he was unable to use these words in front of her, as though she deserved some sort of respect). Even her smile inhibited him. Looking at her closely, he had to admit he had never seen a prettier girl, not so much that she is pretty but that her healthiness, cleanliness, and freshness became increasingly evident. She seemed to have just bathed, that was it, she seemed fresh out of the shower. What would her smell be like? Probably vanilla. She had very straight teeth, which looked gorgeous when she tossed her head back as she laughed. Why did this scandalous woman laugh so much?

"Well then, don't you sometimes feel disgusted with yourself, as though you were a piece of garbage?"

"Me?" she asked in a surprised tone. "Why?"

The judge felt totally disarmed.

"García, go call Lucita so that she can take down the declaration."

Lucita turned out to be the woman with the avocado and banana. She carried her shorthand pad under one arm, her finger still stained with ink. She sat down, grimacing, and muttered, "In her defense, the accused . . ."

"No, wait, take it down directly on the typewriter, it will proceed quicker that way. What do you have to say in your defense, madam Esmeralda?"

"I don't know the legal terminology; I would not know what to say. Why don't you advise me since you are so competent, sir?"

"Th-th-this is it"—the judge stuttered—"now I am supposed to advise her. Read from the file, Lucita."

Lucita opened a file with a white card stuck in the middle and observed: "It isn't signed."

"If you'd like," Esmeralda proposed, "I'll sign it."

"If you haven't declared yet, how could you sign it?"

"It doesn't matter, I will sign first. Anyway, Gabriel told me that the courts put down whatever they want."

"Well your Gabriel is a liar and I am going to have the pleasure of sending him a citation accusing him of defamation."

"Could I see him?" Esmeralda asked happily.

"Gabriel? Well, I really doubt that he would want to place his eyes on you."

"But on the day he comes, would you send for me?"

(This woman is crazy, insane, an animal; all women are crazy—they are vicious, degenerates, demented, beasts. Just look at her, involved with five men at once and still acting fresh as the morning, because this woman doesn't even react to several nights of incarceration nor does she grasp anything that I say, as much as I try to corner her, and to make her understand.) "By then, you will be behind bars in the Santa Marta Acatitla Prison, for desecration of morality, for bigamy, for transgressing social mores" (he flipped through several other crimes in his mind) "for aggravation to particulars, for criminal association, for incitement to rebellion, for attacks on public property. Yes, that too, didn't you and Carlos meet each other in a public park?"

"But, would I be able to see Gabriel?"

"Is Gabriel the one you most adore?" asked the judge, suddenly intrigued.

"No. I love all of them, each one, the same."

"Even Pedro, who denounced you?"

"Oh, my poor little Pedro," she said, shaping her arms as though to cradle a baby near her breast—extremely firm breasts because they remained completely erect while she swung her arms back and forth as though rocking Pedro.

"That's all I needed."

Lucita, with her pencil behind an ear and crunched into her greasy hair, let something like a waxed paper bag crackle between her hands, perhaps so that the judge would become aware of her or so that he would stop yelling. For some time he had kept his eyes intent on the accused, and as a result, four or five employees had arrived to take in each word of the process. Carmelita put aside her comic book, Tere her soaps digest; Carvajal had come to stand alongside García; and Pérez and Mantecón listened without making a sound. Everyone who worked for this courtroom wore a tie but they looked dirty and sweaty, their clothing adhered to them like polyester, their shiny suits full of lint and of that horrible coffee color that darker-skinned people tend to wear, which makes them look like a rancid chocolate bar. Lucita, however, made up for her low stature with strident colors—a green skirt with a nylon yellow blouse, or the opposite. Definite circus combinations, but right now her expression was so enthusiastic she almost looked attractive. Their sparked interest made each appear more noble; they had stopped clomping their feet, scratching, leaning against walls. They were no longer distractedly lazy. Each person came alive, and remembered that they were once men and women, once young, strangers to mounds of paper and white cards to mark places; drops of crystalline water now shone on their foreheads. Esmeralda's presence cleaned them up.

"The newspaper people are outside," Lucita said to the judge.

He immediately rose to his feet. He had a tradition of not detaining the press, the fourth estate. Meanwhile, Lucita moved close to Esmeralda and gave her a pat on the thigh. "Don't worry, sweetie, I'm with you. Your case makes me happy because the bum I married soon had another woman and even put her up in her own place, and here he has me working. So I think it's great that someone like you is mounting revenge. I am going to help you with this last interrogation, I swear on my mother I will help you, sweetie, and not just me, also Carmelita from the desk out front, and Carvajal and Mantecón and Pérez, and Mr. Miguelito, although he's a little old-fashioned he's really a good person, what can I say, for us, you're really worth it. Let's see, I'll begin your declaration: 'The accused declares herself. . . .'" (By that point, Esmeralda, sentenced or not, felt a heavy need of sleep overtake her as she sank down into the chair listening to Lucita's key strokes jubilantly entering all of the proper legal terms, which when written seem totally ominous but spoken out loud were incomprehensible entities, which Lucita diligently communicated out loud to Esmeralda as proof of her loyalty.) At some point, after typing "Bureau of Coordinated Services for Prevention and Social Adaptation," and becoming aware of the absence of acknowledgment from the accused, she leaned over and whispered in her ear:

"You're sleepy, sweetie, but look, we're almost finished. I just have to put in something about the reparation of damages, and make notice to, and reprehension. Oh dear, it doesn't all fit. Well, there it is according to law, be it known that such and such passage of time is required for appeal, expedience, I think that's with an *s*. Anyway, carbon copies to the following, this word needs an accent mark but I did not apply it the previous five times, so it's not that important. Okay, sweetie, here we go, just sign right there and, hey, can I bring you something to drink so that you don't pass out on me?

"This is the formal decree, which presumes guilt; prison time is decreed as well, but don't even worry about it because we won't let it happen. We still need the certified medical report and the notary's seal, the legal conclusions, which are all going to be favorable, you'll see sweetie, I am going to take care of it, you won't have a difficult time."

Once again incarcerated, and after consuming a good broth that included a chicken wing, Esmeralda slept soundly surrounded by sympathetic jailers. The next day, several groups arrived outside the jail to demonstrate in her favor, including the women's sectors of several political parties, and René Cardona Jr., who was insistent about filming a movie based on her life. The journalists had scandalously reported such headlines as "Five, like the fingers on her hand" across eight columns in the police section. In another newspaper, the headline above the fold read, "Five Winners and the Jockey is a Woman," followed by three exclamation points. An editorial writer stated solemnly: "Once again our primitive nature is confronted and tested," followed by additional comments about one's lower instincts. Another writer, obviously a member of the government's cultural program, carried on about the multi-stratification of women's lives, their objectification, their unpaid domestic work that limited their access to paid positions. Other dangerous possibilities were suggested as the reports droned on. It was a tumultuous and tiring day. Among the numerous visitors to the jail were two very agitated nuns, and many other religious women not dressed in robes, all very progressive and almost always French. "Gee," Lucita thought, "what a wondrous day for all women. Although Esmeralda may be punished, she now stands as a symbol for us, making her struggle ours." The judge, upon noticing the heated temperaments of those present, threw cold water on their plans by announcing: "The sentencing will occur behind closed doors."

Lucita nearly disappeared behind the old typewriter and began rewinding the ribbon in its carriage.

"In Iztapalapa, Federal District, at 10:30 A.M. on this 22nd day, within the appointed time period indicated by Article 19 of the Constitution, proceedings for legal resolution were determined in the case of Mrs. Esmeralda Loyden, wife of González, Lugo, Martínez, Mercado, and Vallarta. This court finds her guilty of five counts of adultery, considered as the crime of bigamy, as indicated in Article 37, first paragraph of the Penal Code, backed by Article 122 of the Code for Penal Proceedings. Damages are awarded to the litigant, who in his civil state is called Pedro Lugo Alegría. He filed his protests according to the law so that the truth may be ascertained and subject to legal sanctions. He declared the above to be his name, that he is 32 years of age, married, Catholic, educated, employed, originally from Coatzacoalcos, Veracruz. He declares that on Monday the 28th of May, upon seeing that his wife did not arrive home at the address of

246 Patriotismo, apt. 16, postal code 13, in the neighborhood of San Pedro de los Pinos, as she usually did on Monday at 8 P.M., he went in search of her at the hospital where she said she worked. Upon not finding her there, he asked if she had a shift the following day and was told by the receptionist to check in the main office as she could not find the subject's name on her list, perhaps because she worked a day shift and since this was swing shift she may not be aware of her name, and since it was la" (*la* is all that appeared because Lucita had missed adding the other two letters to spell the word *late*). "As a result he visited the main office and discovered that the person he called his wife never had day, swing, or evening shifts, and as a result the man had to be held down with his arms behind his back, whereupon two emergency room attendants arrived upon being summoned by the office manager, thinking that this man was not in a normal state of mind. Later they saw how this person, now the accuser in this case, left their office staggering, in a terrible state, holding onto the walls because he knew that the person with whom he was sustaining a conjugal relationship was not who she seemed. Afterward the accuser proceeded to employ detectives, as noted in document number 347597, without the knowledge of the accused, and discovered that there were four other men in a similar state as his, and to whom he divulged the quintuplicitous nature of the accused. The presumed penal responsibility for the accused, in the commission of the crimes committed, as charged by Social Representation (an original and five copies, the original for Pedro Lugo Alegría, being as he is the first and principal accuser), is hereby accredited, substantiated by the same elements of proof in the consideration that precedes, with emphasis on the offended party's accusations, and clothing and other personal objects left behind by the accused at each of the five addresses mentioned, as well as the various personal details,

photographic proofs, inscriptions on photographs and other memorabilia, letters and love missives elaborately written by the accused, hereby presented by the aggrieved, and finally, the indisputable authenticity of the marriage certificates, and the consummation of the resulting acts. It can be stated according to the five and the accused herself that the marriages were dutifully and entirely consummated, to complete satisfaction, in the physical person of the wife in each case, one Esmeralda Loyden, who declares herself to be a nurse. That the accused emitted declarations that are not supported by proof of any kind and in effect are disputed by the very elements alluded to"—alluded with two "l"s. "That the accused did not manifest any type of remorse at any time nor did she seem to be aware at any time of the impact of the five charges of which she was accused, that she did not object to anything except for stating that she was sleepy, that the accused was completely docile as she was tested and examined in every way, and thus all necessary exigencies for the clarification of the facts in this case, as required by sections II, IV, and V of Article 20 of the Federal Constitution. All aspects and causes of accusation duly noted and tended to. On the same date, the District Attorney's Office makes note that the time period for all parties to comply with all proof of record begins on the 20th of June and runs to the 12th of July. Sworn and forsworn that the above is true and valid."

As the officiating judge was about to sign his name at the end of the document, he raised his hand and yelled in anger: "Lucita, what on earth is wrong with you? You forgot the 'Effective Suffrage, No Re-Election' again!!"

Right afterward, everything was a blur. Some reported that Esmeralda was led straightaway outside to the waiting jail car, followed by her loyal friend, Lucita, who had prepared her a sandwich for the trip. García, the judge's assistant, kissed her hand, and the judge even gazed affectionately after her as she left. As he said goodbye to her outside, he admonished her as a loving father would, taking both her hands in his, and moving everyone in the crowd with his words: "Esmeralda, see what happens when you deviate so from the traditional path. Listen to me. You're young. Depart from your troubled ways, Esmeralda. Be respectable. From now on, please try to behave properly."

The spectators applauded the convicted woman's dainty steps and gracious manner, which brought a lovely smile to her face. Others, however, witnessed the accuser, Pedro Lugo Alegría, from behind the bars on the car's windows, pierce Esmeralda with his intense gaze. On the other side of the car, the myopic Julio gave her a friendly wave. As she stepped up into the police vehicle, Esmeralda did not see Carlos, but did see Livio, with his head nearly sheared and his eyes in tears. "Why did you cut your long hair, Livio, you know I like it that way." Esmeralda's words were immediately taken down by the journalists. None of the husbands missed the parting, not even the traveling salesman. Authorized accounts have reported that the five husbands had tried to stop the trial because they all wanted Esmeralda back. But since sentencing had already occurred, they were unable to stop the process. They could not even appeal to the Supreme Court of Justice, because the case had received too much publicity; they had to settle for taking turns for conjugal visits at the Santa Marta Acatitla Prison. But of course, it was much the same schedule they had enjoyed previously, *de facto et in situ*, since they had only seen her one night per week before the trial. In fact, they quite often gathered all together for the Sunday general-day visits, each bringing a different delectable treat, which was enjoyed not only by Esmeralda, but also Lucita, Carmelita, Tere, García, Carvajal, Pérez, Mantecón, and even the judge himself, who had become addicted to Esmeralda's sweet responses.

This case, however, cannot be consulted in the public record, since the accusers and the accused, the judge, and other officials all repented of having hastily mounted the first formal decree, number 479-32-875746, page 68, and everything remained instead in the so-called Book of Life, which is quite *cursi* and which preceded the book currently used to inscribe facts; its ugly name is: computer documentation. I hereby swear and forswear that this document is true and valid. Effective Suffrage, No Re-Election.

HALIW   PONIA

PONIATOWSKA, ELENA
    LILUS KIKUS AND OTHER
    STORIES
ALIEF
06/06